*My Life in
the Bush of Ghosts*

ALSO BY AMOS TUTUOLA
Published by Grove Weidenfeld

The Palm-Wine Drinkard

My Life in
the Bush of Ghosts

by

AMOS TUTUOLA

with a foreword
by

The Rev. Geoffrey Parrinder, D.D., Ph.D.
*Lecturer at University College, Ibadan,
Nigeria*

GROVE WEIDENFELD
New York

Published by Grove Weidenfeld
A division of Wheatland Corporation
841 Broadway
New York, NY 10003-4793

ISBN: 0-8021-3105-0

Library of Congress Catalog Card Number 54-12101

Manufactured in the United States of America

Printed on acid-free paper

First Evergreen Edition 1970

10 9 8

Contents

7

Contents

Foreword

When Amos Tutuola's first novel, *The Palm-Wine Drinkard*, was published in 1952 it was presented to the public without introduction and made its way purely on its merit. Considerable interest was aroused by this unusual book, and inquiries have been made about Tutuola and the background of his ideas. It has been thought well to preface this second novel with a few words about the man and his work, in order that his importance may be appreciated in its proper setting.

Amos Tutuola is a native of Abeokuta, one of the big towns of Nigeria, in West Africa. He is a member of the large Yoruba tribe, which numbers over four million people and is one of the most progressive elements in modern Africa. Abeokuta, whose name means "under the rock", is a large sprawling town situated along the sides of hills which are crowned with masses of granite boulders. It is a medley of old mud huts and new concrete buildings, a mixture of cultures such as the subject-matter of the books would lead us to expect. Alongside the modern mosques and churches are ancient pagan temples, and a cave under the most sacred rock is said to have witnessed a human sacrifice as recently as forty years ago. Twice in the present book the wanderer in the bush of ghosts is to be sacrificed to a god.

9

Foreword

Amos Tutuola was born in 1920, of Christian parents, and he received elementary education at the Salvation Army school and later at Lagos High School, not more than six years in all. He became a coppersmith, and continued this trade in the Royal Air Force in Nigeria for three years during the war.

Tutuola's writing is original and highly imaginative. His direct style, made more vivid by his use of English as it is spoken in West Africa, is not polished or sophisticated and gives his stories unusual energy. It is a beginning of a new type of Afro-English literature. Tutuola prefers to write in English, rather than Yoruba; it is perhaps fortunate that his schooling ended too early to force his story-telling into a foreign style. His writing is distinct from the correct but rather stiff essays that some more highly educated Africans produce. Tutuola's stories are of the kind, lively, vulgar, frightening, which is common in the traditional Africa of the villages.

This story is truly African. It is a fantasy, shaped by the author's fertile imagination. It has a nightmarish quality of its own, and one feels the bewilderment and fear, repugnance and despair, and also intoxication and exaltation, which one would expect to experience in the company of ghosts. But the stories are genuine African myths, such as are told in countless villages round the fire or in the tropical moonlight. Africans have said to me, "My grandmother used to tell us stories like that." Tutuola has told me how he and his boyhood playmates would listen to such yarns on their farms in the evening.

Amos Tutuola has taken over the traditional mythology

10

and fitted it into his own pattern. There is an over-riding theme: what happens to a mortal who strays into the world of ghosts. This is a familiar motif. Into this have been worked popular beliefs, such as that in the "Burglar-ghosts" who are children that die in infancy and are reborn again and again, and are really troublesome ghosts come to plague and rob the unhappy parents. Again there is "Lost or Gain Valley", which has to be crossed without clothes, but it is a riddle that might be capable of solution. Elsewhere we find witches meeting to devour a victim provided from the family of one of their company. Yet all these ideas are moulded into the story and are lived over by the author. I realized how deeply he lived in his own narrative when I asked Tutuola the reason for the apparently haphazard order of the towns of the ghosts. He replied, quite simply, "That is the order in which I came to them."

From the second chapter, where the lost boy is beckoned on by the Golden-ghost, the Silverish-ghost, and the Copperish-ghost, captured by the disgusting Smelling-ghost, transformed into a horse and later a cow, and then caught by a Homeless-ghost, one is impelled on through all the bizarre adventures. One goes with the author in his waking nightmare. Fear is present throughout. If anyone doubts that there is fear in African life Tutuola's story should convince him of its reality. The unknown bush with its frightful spirits stretching out their tentacles, like trees in an Arthur Rackham drawing, is a dreadful place. Fairy tales can scare, but this is more terrifying than Grimm as its matter is more serious and is believed in by millions of Africans today.

11

Foreword

The "Bush" in which the ghosts live is the heart of the tropical forest, the impenetrable thickets that are left even when the rest of the forest is cleared for cultivation. Here, as every hunter and traveller knows, mortals venture at their peril. Nobody dares enter there by day, let alone go near at night. In another manuscript Tutuola says that, in addition to the Reserved and Unreserved Bush specified by the government, there is Native Reserved Bush. "It is strictly out of bounds to both Whites and Blacks, because it is only for dead Ghosts and bad Juju. . . . If you enter into it you cannot know the way out again, and you cannot travel to the end of it for ever."

Readers of *The Palm-Wine Drinkard* will remember Deads' Town, where are the spirits of the departed. The ghosts in the present book are different from those deceased mortals. They are all types of beings who have never lived on earth and are dangerous and mischievous spirits. They are creatures of God but different from men; they never grow old or die. Dead people can indeed live with them, and we meet two such, but these are ones who have died before their time and so can live with the ageless spirits.

At the same time as it relates old themes, the story reflects the situation of Africans under the impact of European ideas and government. The ancient beliefs still prevail in this mythology, but they are impregnated by modern touches. So we find churches, schools and Crown Agents in the 10th Town of Ghosts, and the Rev. Devil giving a baptism of fire and hot water in the 8th Town. Later we have a Television-handed Ghostess, described by a man who has never seen television.

Foreword

This book is fascinating from the point of view of pure story. It also has scientific value. The anthropologist and the student of comparative religion will find here much of the unrecorded mythology of West Africa. There are themes running through the book, as to the nature of death, fear and disease. There are discernible stages in the process of initiation into the mysteries of the ghost-world, which link up with the rites of secret societies and religious cults. The wanderer in the bush, after his grim early sufferings, gradually learns the language of ghosts and marries two ghosts. He remains twenty-four years in the bush, until he has almost lost the desire to return.

Further, the work is an interesting example of "culture-contact", which is just as much the student's province today as was the "unspoiled native" yesterday. How far have Christian ideas penetrated? Have they changed or displaced ancient beliefs? This book goes some way towards providing an answer. The student is concerned with the African as he is today, as a human being, to understand whom is as important for an imperial people as it is to understand Russians or Americans. We now know a great deal about African economy, social organization, political structure, and their modification in this century, but how hard it is to understand the thoughts of other races, even of those who resemble us superficially, and much more of those whose traditions have been so widely separated from our own.

Psychologists will find this book interesting, particularly those who follow the teaching of Jung on mythology and the archetypes of the unconscious. The morbid fascination of dirt, blood, snakes, insects, smell, ugliness, deformity, size, and all that is grotesque is everywhere evident in the book. The lost boy undergoes more transformations in size and form than Alice in Wonderland. In the midst of his greatest distress and captivity he is so intoxicated by the fumes of the gigantic tobacco pipe that he is forced to smoke, that "I forgot all my sorrow and started to sing the earthly songs which sorrow prevented me from singing about since I entered this bush." In great danger of pursuit he is so entranced by the exceeding ugliness of a ghostess, that he is impelled to delay and look at her face, "her ugly appearance was so curious to me that I was chasing her as she was running away to see her ugliness clearly to my satisfaction". In the end the boy comes to settle in the ghost world so well that, like Persephone, he is reluctant to leave it; "I did not feel to go to my town again, even I determined that I should not go for ever." When he does at length find the way, the return is easy and immediate. But we are warned that he has premonitory dreams of attendance at the coming centenary of the Secret Society of Ghosts.

My Life in the Bush of Ghosts was written after *The Palm-Wine Drinkard*. It is in no sense a sequel, but a completely new story. It deals not with "Deads", but with the spirits of the wild. These abnormal beings remind one of the creations of Bunyan and Dante. The story is a coherent whole and the closing sentence, "This is what hatred did", links up with the opening chapter wherein are revealed the jealousies of a polygamous household which leave a small boy, who does not know what is "good" or "bad", to face by himself the terrors of the Bush of Ghosts.

Foreword

The book has been edited to remove the grosser
mistakes, clear up some ambiguities, and curtail some
repetition. But the original flavour of the style has been
left to produce its own effect.

University College,   GEOFFREY PARRINDER
Ibadan, Nigeria

The Meaning of
"Bad" and "Good"

I was seven years old before I understood the meaning of "bad" and "good", because it was at that time I noticed carefully that my father married three wives as they were doing in those days, if it is not common nowadays. My mother was the last married among the rest and she only bore two sons but the rest bore only daughters. So by that the two wives who had only daughters hated my mother, brother and myself to excess as they believed that no doubt my brother and myself would be the rulers of our father's house and also all his properties after his death. My brother was eleven years old then and I myself was seven. So it was at this stage I quite understood the meaning of "bad" because of hatred and had not yet known the meaning of "good".

My mother was a petty trader who was going to various markets every day to sell her articles and returning home in the evening, or if the market is very far she would return next day in the evening as she was a hard worker.

In those days of unknown year, because I was too young to keep the number of the year in my mind till this time, so there were many kinds of African wars and some of them are as follows: general wars, tribal wars, burglary wars and the slave wars which were very common in every town and village and particularly in famous markets and on main roads of big towns at any time in the day or night. These slave-wars were causing dead luck to both old and young of those days, because if one is captured, he or she would be sold into slavery for foreigners who would carry him or her to unknown destinations to be killed for the buyer's god or to be working for him.

But as my mother was a petty trader who was going here and there, so one morning she went to a market which was about three miles away from our town, she left two slices of cooked yam for us (my brother and myself) as she was usually doing. When it was twelve o'clock p.m. cocks began to crow continuously, then my brother and myself entered into our mother's room in which she kept the two sliced or cut yams safely for us, so that it might not be poisoned by the two wives who hated us, then my brother took one of the yams and I took the other one and began to eat it at the same time. But as we were eating the yam inside our mother's room, these two wives who hated us heard information before us that war was nearly breaking into the town, so both of them and their daughters ran away from the town without informing us or taking us along with themselves and all of them knew already that our mother was out of the town.

Even as we were very young to know the meaning of "bad" and "good" both of us were dancing to the noises of the enemies' guns which were reverberating into the room in which we were eating the yam as the big trees and many hills with deep holes on them entirely sur-

18

rounded the town and they changed the fearful noises of the enemies' guns to a lofty one for us, and we were dancing for these lofty noises of the enemies' guns.

But as these enemies were more approaching the town the lofty noises of their guns became fearful for us because every place was shaking at that moment. So when we could not bear it then we left our mother's room for thé veranda, but we met nobody there, and then we ran from there to the portico of the house, but the town was also empty except the domestic animals as sheep, pigs, goats and fowls and also some of the bush animals as monkeys, wolves, deer and lions who were driven from the bush that surrounded the town to the town by the fearful noises of the enemies' guns. All these animals were running and crying bitterly up and down in the town in searching for their keepers. Immediately we saw that there was nobody in the town again we stepped down from the door to the outside as all the while we stood at the door looking at every part of the town with fearful and doubtful mind.

So first of all we travelled to the north of the town as there was a road which led to the town of our grandmother which was not far away from ours.

But as these animals were giving us much trouble, fear, and disturbing us so at last we left to run to the north and then to the south where there was a large river which crossed the road on which we should travel to some protective place to hide ourselves.

And as the enemies were approaching nearer, we left the river at once and when we went further on this road we reached a kind of African fruit tree which stood by

19

the road, then we stopped under it to find a shelter, but as we were hastily turning round this tree perhaps we would see a shelter there, two ripe fruits fell down on it, then my brother took both and put them into his pocket and started to carry or lift me along on this road as I was too young to run as fast as he could. But as he himself was too young to lift or carry such weight like me, so by that he was unable to lift me to a distance of about ten feet before he would fall down four times or more.

When he tried all his power for several times and failed and again at that moment the smell of the gunpowder of the enemies' guns which were shooting repeatedly was rushing to our noses by the breeze and this made us fear more, so my brother lifted me again a very short distance, but when I saw that he was falling several times, then I told him to leave me on the road and run away for his life perhaps he might be safe so that he would be taking care of our mother as she had no other sons more than both of us and I told him that if God saves my life too then we should meet again, but if God does not save my life we should meet in heaven.

But as I was telling him these sorrowful words both his eyes were shedding tears repeatedly, of course I did not shed tears at all on my eyes as I put hope that no doubt I would be easily captured or killed. And it was that day I believed that if fear is overmuch, a person would not fear for anything again. But as the smoke of the enemies' guns was rushing to our view, then my brother left me on that road with sorrow, and then he stopped and put his hand into his pocket and brought out the fruits which fell down from the tree under which we were about to hide ourselves before; he gave me both fruits instead of one. After that he started to run as fast as he could along this road towards the enemies unnoticed and he was still looking at me as he was running away.

So after I saw him no more on the road I put both fruits into my pocket and then got back to that fruit tree under which we picked them and I stood there only to shelter myself from the sun. But when the enemies were at a distance of about an eighth of a mile to that place where I stood I was unable to hear again because of the noises of the enemies' guns and as I was too young to hear such fearful noises and wait, so I entered into the bush under this fruit tree. This fruit tree was a "SIGN" for me and it was on that day I called it—THE "FUTURE SIGN".

Now it remained me alone in the bush, because no brother, mother, father or other defender could save me or direct me if and whenever any danger is imminent. But as these enemies had approached us closely before my brother left because of me he was captured within fifteen minutes that he left me, but he was only captured as a slave and not killed, because I heard his voice when he shouted louder for help.

In the Bush of Ghosts

At the same time as I entered into the bush I could not stop in one place as the noises of the guns were driving me farther and farther until I travelled about sixteen miles away from the road on which my brother left me. After I had travelled sixteen miles and was still running further for the fearful noises, I did not know the time that I entered into a dreadful bush which is called the "Bush of Ghosts", because I was very young to understand the meaning of "bad" and "good". This "Bush of Ghosts" was so dreadful so that no superior earthly person ever entered it.

But as the noises of the enemies' guns drove me very far until I entered into the "Bush of Ghosts" unnoticed, because I was too young to know that it was a dreadful bush or it was banned to be entered by any earthly person, so that immediately I entered it I stopped and ate both fruits which my brother gave me before we left each other, because I was very hungry before I reached there. After I ate it then I started to wander about in this bush both day and night until I reached a rising ground which was almost covered with thick bush and weeds which made the place very dark both day and night. Every part of this small hill was very clean as if somebody was sweeping it. But as I was very tired of roaming about before I reached there, so I bent down to see the hill clearly, because my aim was to sleep there. Yet I could not see it clearly as I bent down, but when I had lain down flatly then I saw clearly that it had an entrance with which to enter into it.

The entrance resembled the door of a house and it had a portico which was sparkling as if it was polished with brasso at all moments. The portico was also made of golden plate. But as I was too young to know "bad" and "good" I thought that it was an old man's house who was expelled from a town for an offence, then I entered it and went inside it until I reached a junction of three passages which each led to a room as there were three rooms.

One of these rooms had golden surroundings, the second had silverish surroundings and the third had copperish. But as I stood at the junction of these passages with confusion three kinds of sweet smells were rushing out to me from each of these three rooms, but as I was hungry and also starving before I entered into this hole, so I began to sniff the best smell so that I might enter the right room at once from which the best sweet smell was rushing out. Of course as I stood on this junction I noticed through my nose that the smell which was rushing out of the room which had golden surroundings was just as if the inhabitant of it was baking bread and roasting fowl, and when I sniffed again the smell of the room which had copperish surroundings was just as if the inhabitant of that was cooking rice, potatoes and other African food with very sweet soup, and then the room which had silverish surroundings was just as if the inhabitant was frying yam, roasting fowl and baking cakes. But I thought in my mind to go direct to the room from which the smell of the African food was rushing out to me, as I prefer my native food most. But I did not know that all that I was thinking in mind was going to the hearing of the inhabitants of these three rooms, so at the same moment that I wanted to move my body to go to the room from which the smell of the African's food was rushing to me (the room which had copperish surroundings) there I saw that these three rooms which had no doors and windows opened unexpectedly and three kinds of ghosts peeped at me, every one of them pointed his finger to me to come to him.

These ghosts were so old and weary that it is hard to believe that they were living creatures. Then I stood at this junction with my right foot which I dangled with fear and looking at them. But as I was looking at each of them surprisingly I noticed that the inhabitant of the room which had golden surroundings was a golden ghost in appearance, then the second room which had copperish surroundings was a copperish ghost and also the third was a silverish ghost.

As every one of them pointed his finger to me to come to him I preferred most to go direct to the copperish-ghost from whose room the smell of African's food was rushing out to me, but when the golden ghost saw my movement which showed that I wanted to go to the copperish-ghost, so at the same time he lighted the golden flood of light all over my body to persuade me not to go to the copperish-ghost, as every one of them wanted me to be his servant. So as he lighted the flood of golden light on my body and when I looked at myself I thought

24

that I became gold as it was shining on my body, so at this time I preferred most to go to him because of his golden light. But as I moved forward a little bit to go to him then the copperish-ghost lighted the flood of his own copperish light on my body too, which persuaded me again to go to the golden-ghost as my body was changing to every colour that copper has, and my body was then so bright so that I was unable to touch it. And again as I preferred this copperish light more than the golden-light then I started to go to him, but at this stage I was prevented again to go to him by the silverish-light which shone on to my body at that moment unexpectedly. This silverish-light was as bright as snow so that it trans-parented every part of my body and it was this day I knew the number of the bones of my body. But immedi-ately I started to count them these three ghosts shone the three kinds of their lights on my body at the same time in such a way that I could not move to and fro because of these lights. But as these three old ghosts shone their lights on me at the same time so I began to move round as a wheel at this junction, as I appreciated these lights as the same.

But as I was staggering about on this junction for about half an hour because of these lights, the copperish-ghost was wiser than the rest, he quenched his own copperish-light from my body, so at this time I had a little chance to go to the rest. Of course, when the golden-ghost saw that I could not run two races at a blow success-fully, so he quenched his own light too from my body, and at this time I had chance to run a single race to the silverish-ghost. But when I nearly reached his room then

the copperish-ghost and the golden-ghost were lighting
their lights on me as signals and at the same moment the
silverish-ghost joined them to use his own light as signal
to me as well, because I was disturbed by the other two
ghosts. Then I stopped again and looking at every one of
them how he was shining his own lights on me at two or
three seconds' interval as signal.

Although I appreciated or recognized these lights as
the same, but I appreciated one thing more which is
food, and this food is my native food which was cooked by
the copperish-ghost, but as I was very hungry so I
entered into his room, and when he saw that it was his
room I entered he was exceedingly glad so that he gave
me the food which was the same colour with copper. But
as every one of these three old ghosts wanted me to be
his servant, so that the other two ghosts who were the
golden-ghost and the silverish-ghost did not like me to
be servant for the copperish-ghost who gave me the food
that I preferred most, and both entered into the room of
the copperish-ghost, all of them started to argue. At last
all of them held me tightly in such a way that I could not
breathe in or out. But as they held me with argument for
about three hours, so when I was nearly cut into three as
they were pulling me about in the room I started to cry
louder so that all the ghosts and ghostesses of that area
came to their house and within twenty minutes this
house could not contain the ghosts who heard information
and came to settle the misunderstanding. But when they
came and met them how they were pulling me about in
the room with much argument then they told them to
leave me and they left me at once.

In the Bush of Ghosts

After that all the ghosts who came to settle the matter arranged these three old ghosts in a single line and then they told me to choose one of them for myself to be my master so that there would be no more misunderstanding between themselves. So I stood before them and looking at every one of them with my heart which was throbbing hastily to the hearing of all of them, in such a way that the whole of the ghosts who came to settle the matter rushed to me to listen well to what my heart was saying. But as these wonderful creatures understood what my heart was saying they warned me not to choose any one of them with my mouth, because they thought it would speak partiality against one of these three ghosts, as my heart was throbbing repeatedly as if a telegraphist is sending messages by telegraph.

As a matter of fact my heart first told me to choose the silverish-ghost who stood at the extreme right and if to say I would choose by mouth I would only choose the copperish-ghost who had the African's food and that was partiality, and it was at this time I noticed carefully all the ghosts who came to settle the matter that many of them had no hands and some had no fingers, some had no feet and arms but jumped instead of walking. Some had heads without eyes and ears, but I was very surprised to see them walking about both day and night without missing their way and also it was this day I had ever seen ghosts without clothes on their bodies and they were not ashamed of their nakedness.

Uncountable numbers of them stood before me and looked at me as dolls with great surprise as they had no heads or eyes. But as they forced me to choose the silverish-ghost as he was the ghost that my heart throbbed out to their hearing to choose, when I chose him, he was exceedingly glad and ran to me, then he took me on his shoulder and then to his room. But still the other two were not satisfied with the judgement of the settlers and both ran to his room and started to fight again. This fight was so fearful and serious that all the creatures in that bush with big trees stood still on the same place that they were, even breezes could not blow at this time and these three old ghosts were still fighting on fiercely until a fearful ghost who was almost covered with all kinds of insects which represented his clothes entered their house when hearing their noises from a long distance.

The Smelling-Ghost

All kinds of snakes, centipedes and flies were living on every part of his body. Bees, wasps and uncountable mosquitoes were also flying round him and it was hard to see him plainly because of these flies and insects. But immediately this dreadful ghost came inside this house from heaven-knows-where his smell and also the smell of his body first drove us to a long distance before we came back after a few minutes, but still the smell did not let every one of the settlers stand still as all his body was full of excreta, urine, and also wet with the rotten blood of all the animals that he was killing for his food. His mouth which was always opening, his nose and eyes were very hard to look at as they were very dirty and smelling. His name is "Smelling-ghost". But what made me surprised and fear most was that this "smelling-ghost" wore many scorpions on his fingers as rings and all were alive, many poisonous snakes were also on his neck as beads and he belted his leathern trousers with a very big and long boa constrictor which was still alive.

Of course at first I did not know that he was the king of all the smelling-ghosts in the 7th town of ghosts. Immediately he entered this house, they (golden-ghost, silverish-ghost and copperish-ghost) stopped fighting at once. After that he called them out of the room in which they were fighting, when they came out and stood before him, then he asked for the matter, but when they told him he called me out of the room in which I hid myself for his bad smell with his fearful appearance which I was dreaming of, without sleeping. When they called me to come to him and when I stood before him I closed my eyes, mouth and nose with both my hands because of his smell. Then he told them that he would cut me into three parts and give each part to each of them so that there would be no more misunderstanding. But as I heard from him that he would cut me into three, I fainted more than an hour before my heart came back to normal.

But God is so good these three old ghosts were not satisfied with his judgement at all, and after they had rested for a few minutes, they started fighting again.

So I was very lucky as they did not agree for him to cut me for them and when he saw that they did not agree but were still fighting, then he gripped me with his hands which were very hot and put me into the big bag which he hung on his left shoulder and kept going away at the same time. But when he threw me into the bag I was totally covered with the rotten blood of the animals which he was killing in the bush. This bag was so smelling and full of mosquitoes, small snakes with centipedes which did not let me rest for a moment. This is how I left the golden-ghost, silverish-ghost and copperish-ghost and it was from their house I started my punishment in this "Bush of Ghosts". After he left these three ghosts and travelled till the evening, then he stopped suddenly, thinking within himself with a loud voice either to eat me or to eat half of me and reserve the other half till night. Because as he was taking me along in the bush he was trying all his best to kill a bush animal to eat as food, as he could not reach his town which is the 7th town of smelling-ghosts on that day.

Although as he was carrying me along in the bush he was trying his best to kill the animals, his bad smell was suspecting him that he was coming so they were running away before he could reach them. He could not kill an animal unless it sleeps. But as I was hearing him when he was discussing either to eat me, luckily an animal was passing at that time, then he started to chase it until he saw a half-dead animal which was totally helpless, so he stopped there and began to eat it voraciously and to my surprise he was also cutting some of the animal into pieces and giving them to all the snakes etc. which were on every part of his body. After he was satisfied with this animal, then he put the rest together with its blood into the bag and it fell on to my head as a heavy load. After that he got up and kept going. But as he was travelling along in the bush and as all the snakes on his body were not satisfied with the meat before him they were rushing to the inside of the bag and eating the meat which he threw into the bag and then rushing out at the same time so that he might not suspect them. Sometimes they were mistakenly biting me several times as they could not hesitate for suspicion of their boss who might punish them for stealing. But once I heard from him when discussing within himself whether to eat me before an animal was passing I planned to stretch my hand out from the bag and hold the branch of a gravity tree, as he was sometimes creeping under the lower bush to a distance of a mile or more; this plan means to escape from him.

But after he had travelled for two hours, I noticed that it was very dark, then I got up from the bag to peep out and hold the branch of a gravity tree, because if I jumped right out from the bag he would suspect or remember that I was inside the bag, as I thought that perhaps he had forgotten me there and perhaps if he catches me again at that time he would remember to eat me. Harder to stay in the bag and hardest to come out of it because when it was very dark I got up to peep out and look for the branch of a tree to hold as he was going on, but as these snakes were always rushing in and out of this bag so that at the same time that they saw me they wanted to eat me too as the meat, then I cast down inside the bag at the same moment, and after a few minutes later I peeped out again and they drove me back again, even I could not wait and breathe in fresh air.

So they disallowed me to do as I planned until he reached a place where other kinds of ghosts were in conference, then he stopped and sat with them, but he sat on me as there was no more stool.

As they were discussing some important matters for some hours, he got up on me and took out the rest meat from the bag, he put it before the ghosts that he met there and the whole of them started to eat it together. At that time I was praying not to remember to present me to these ghosts as that meat, until a lower rank ghost brought a very big animal and gave them as a present. But as he sat on me it was hard for me to breathe in or out and if it was not for the boa constrictor with which he belted his trousers which was made with the skin of an animal, I would die for his weight as I could not raise him up or lift him up at all. When it was about two o'clock in the midnight their meeting closed and then every one of them started to go to his town. After the meeting had closed he got up from me and hung the bag back on his shoulder and then kept going to his town. But as he was going hastily along in the bush all the animals were running very far away for his bad smell whenever he met them. If he was at a distance of four miles from a creature it would suspect him through his powerful smell. I was still inside this bag until he reached his town which is 7th town of ghosts on the third day.

My Life in the 7th Town of Ghosts

When he reached his town and entered his house then he took me out of the bag and I saw clearly that all his family were also smelling, and his house was smelling so that immediately he took me out from the bag I was unable to breathe out for thirty minutes. The most wonderful thing I noticed carefully in this smelling town was that all the babies born the same day were also smelling as a dead animal. This smelling town was separated and very far away from all other towns of ghosts. If any one of these smelling-ghosts touched anything it would become a bad smell at the same moment and it is bad luck for any ghost who is not a native of smelling-ghosts to meet a smelling-ghost on the way when going somewhere. It is also very bad luck for a smelling-ghost if he meets any other kind of ghosts on the way if his bad smell does not drive them very far away. At the same time as he took me out of the bag he gave me food which I was unable to eat as it was smelling badly. But as I was unable to eat this food I asked for water as I never drank water since I left my brother or since I entered into the "Bush of Ghosts", but they gave me urine as it was their water which they were storing in a big pot, of course I refused to drink it as well. There I noticed in this house

34

that mosquitoes, wasps, flies of all kinds and all kinds of poisonous snakes were disturbing them from walking easily about and it was as dark in the day as in the night, so this darkness enabled uncountable snakes to fill up there as if they were taming or keeping them.

It was in this town I saw that they had an "Exhibition of Smells". All the ghosts of this town and environs were assembling yearly and having a special "Exhibition of Smells" and the highest prizes were given to one who had the worst smells and would be recognized as a king since that day as all of them were appreciating dirt more than clean things.

When it was night he pushed me with all his power into one of the rooms which were in his house, and I met uncountable flies, snakes and all other kinds of pest creatures which drove me back at the same time as he pushed me in, but as these pest creatures drove me back to him, then he pushed me to them again and closed the door of the room. Immediately he pushed me back to them and closed the door I was covered by these pest creatures and it was hard for me to move about in this room. When I laid down to sleep on the floor without a mat I asked for a cover-cloth to cover my body, perhaps the smells would allow me to sleep or to breathe, but when all of them heard cover-cloth, they exclaimed: what is called—"cover-cloth". Of course, when they said so, I remembered that I was not with my mother or in my town. I could not sleep or rest for a minute till morning because of these pest creatures, and also the bad smells which were blowing from everywhere to this room or house. But when I got out from this room in the morning to the veranda I met over two thousand smelling-ghosts who came from various provinces of this 7th town of ghosts which was the capital to greet him for his good luck, because it was good luck for my boss as he brought me to his house or town.

Immediately I got out from the room they told me to sit down in their middle as they sat down in a circle, so all of them surrounded me closely and looking at me with much astonishment as I was breathing once a minute because of their smells which they themselves were enjoying as perfume or lavender.

In the presence of these guests, my boss was changing me to some kinds of creatures. First of all he changed me to a monkey, then I began to climb fruit trees and pluck fruits down for them. After that he changed me to a lion, then to a horse, to a camel, to a cow or bull with horns on its head and at last to my former form. Having finished that, his wives who were all the while cooking all kinds of food brought the food to them together with ghosts' drinks at the same place that they sat, and looking at me as dolls, because none of them had ever seen an earthly person in his or her life. None of them talked a single word, as looking at me motionless as dolls and all these food and drinks were also smelling badly, and at the same time that they brought them it was hard to see what sort of food and drinks because of flies which almost covered them. After all of them had eaten and drunk to their entire satisfaction then they were dancing the ghosts' dance round me and beating drums, clapping hands on me and singing the song of ghosts with gladness until a late hour in the night before every one of them

who came from various provinces of this 7th town returned to his or her province and those who came from
this 7th town returned to their houses. But he was still
receiving uncountable messages, congratulations with
many presents from those who were too old or in difficulties to present themselves at this "good luck ceremony".

After the fourth day that he had performed the "lucky-
ceremony", his oldest son, who had only an arm and had
no teeth in his mouth, with a bare head which was
sparkling as if it was polished, took me out of the house
to the front house. After that his father came and
performed a juju which changed me to a horse unexpectedly, then he put reins into my mouth and tied me
on a stump with a thick rope, after this he went back to
the house and dressed in a big cloth which was made with
a kind of ghosts' leaves which was the most expensive
and he was only entitled to use such an expensive cloth
as he is the king of all the smelling-ghosts, but all these
smelling-ghosts did not appreciate earthly clothes as
anything. After a while he came out with two of his
attendants who were following him to wherever he
wanted to go. Then the attendants loosened me from the
stump, so he mounted me and the two attendants were
following him with whips in their hands and flogging me
along in the bush. As he was dressed with these leaves and
mounted me mercilessly I felt as if he was half a ton
weight.

Then he was riding me to the towns of those who
attended and who were unable to attend his "lucky-
ceremony" to greet them and whenever he reached a
house he would get down off me and enter the house to

greet the owner of it who came and enjoyed the "lucky-ceremony" with him or who sent him presents. But within an hour that he entered and left the attendants with me all the rest of the young ghosts and old ghosts of that area would surround me and look at me with great surprise. Sometimes these young or children ghosts would be touching my eyes with their fingers or sticks, so that perhaps I would feel it or cry and they would hear how my voice would be. He spent almost one hour in any house he was entering, because he would eat and drink together with everyone that he was visiting to their satisfaction before the whole of them would come out and look at me for about half an hour. After that he would mount me mercilessly and both his attendants would start to flog me in such a way that all the ghosts and ghostesses of that town would shout at me as a thief. But if they shouted at me like that my boss would jump and kick me mercilessly, with gladness in the presence of these bystanders until he would leave that town.

When it was two o'clock in the midday, he reached a village which also belonged to the smelling-town, he got down from me and entered the largest and finest house which belonged to the head of this village, and after a few minutes that he had entered the house a fearful ghost who was speaking with his nose and whose belly was on his thighs brought horse's food in which guinea corn and many leaves were included to me. But as I had never eaten anything since my boss took me from the three old ghosts so by that I ate the corn which I had never tasted since I was born, but I was unable to eat the leaves as I am not really a horse. Having finished the corn another terrible ghost whose eyes were watering all over his body and his large mouth faced his back brought urine which was mixed with limestone to me to drink as they were not using ordinary water there because it is too clean for them. But as I was all the while tied in the sun which was shining severely on me, then I tasted it as I was exceedingly feeling thirsty, although I took off my mouth at once when I discovered that it was urine and limestone. And the worst part of these punishments was that as I was tied in the sun all the young ghosts of this village were mounting me and getting down as if I am a tree as they were very surprised to see me as a horse.

When it was about eight o'clock in the night my boss came out from that house together with some prominent ghosts of the village and after they looked at me for some minutes he hung all the presents given to him on me and then mounted me. As it was very dark at that time, so I was staggering or dashing into trees along the way when he was returning to his town, and it was almost one o'clock midnight before we reached his town. Having reached his home he was unable to change me to my former form that night, but his attendants simply tied me on a stump outside as he drank too much. So the whole of them left me there and I was totally covered by mosquitoes until morning but had no hands to drive them away. But he came in the morning and changed me to my former form.

After some minutes he gave me their smelling food which I was unable to eat satisfactorily. But after I ate some of this food he changed me again to the form of a

39

camel and then his sons were using me as transport to carry heavy loads to long distances of about twenty or forty miles. But when the rest of the smelling-ghosts noticed that I was useful for such purpose then the whole of them were hiring me from my boss to carry loads to long distances and returning again in the evening with heavier loads. But as I could not satisfy all of them at a time so they shared me, half of them would use me from morning till night, then the rest would use me from the night till morning. At this stage I had no chance to rest for a minute for all the periods that I spent with them.

As the news had been spread to many towns of other kinds of ghosts, and as all of them wanted to see me as a horse, so they invited my boss to a conference so that they might see how he would ride me to their town where the conference would be held, because ghosts like to be in conference at all times. But as he ought to change me from the camel to a horse, because the camel is useful only to carry loads so by that he changed me to a person as I was all the while in form of a camel. After he changed me to a person then he went away to take the reins which he would put into my mouth when he changed me to a horse, but as soon as he went away I saw where he hid the juju which he was using to change me to any animal or creature that he likes, so I took it and put it into my pocket so that he might not change me to anything again. God is so good, he did not remember to take the juju when he came out from the house, he thought that he had already put it inside the pocket of his leathern trousers which he was always belting with a big boa constrictor, because he would not change me to a horse until he

40

climbed a mountain which was at a distance of about six miles from his town and his aim was that he would change me to a horse after he had climbed the mountain and ride me from there to the town in which he was invited to the conference.

When he came back from the house he simply threw me inside the big bag which he hung on his shoulder, because he could not go anywhere without this bag, as it is a uniform for every king that reigns in this 7th town of ghosts which belongs only to smelling-ghosts. Immediately he put me inside the bag then he kept going to the town that they invited him to. But when he climbed the mountain to the top he branched to his right then he bent down and started to pass excreta. But as I was inside the bag I was thinking how I could escape from him, and after a while I remembered that I had taken the juju which he would use before he could change me to any creature that he likes and at this time he has no power to change me to a horse again. So I jumped right out from the bag to the ground and without hesitation I started to run away inside the bush for my life and immediately he saw me running away he got up and started to chase me, saying thus with loud voice: "Ah! the earthly person is running away, how can I catch him now, oh! what can I ride on to the conference today, as all the ghosts who invited me are waiting to see me on a horse. Oh! if I had known I should have changed him to a horse before I left home. But if my head helps me and I catch him now I will change him from today to a permanent horse for ever. Ah! how can I catch him now?" But as he was chasing me fiercely and saying like that, I myself was

41

also saying thus: "Ah! how can I save myself from this smelling-ghost who wants to catch me and change me to a permanent horse for ever, and if he catches me now it means I would not return to my town or I will not see my mother for ever?"

But as any ghost could run faster than any earthly person, so that I became tired before him, and when he was about to catch me or when his hand was touching my head slightly to catch it, then I used the juju which I took from the hidden place that he kept it in before we left his house. And at the same moment that I used it, it changed me to a cow with horns on its head instead of a horse, but I forgot before I used it that I would not be able to change back to the earthly person again, because I did not know another juju which he was using before changing me back to an earthly person. Of course as I had changed to a cow I became more powerful and started to run faster than him, but still, he was chasing me fiercely until he became tired. And when he was about to go back from me I met a lion again who was hunting up and down in the bush at that time for his prey as he was very hungry, and without hesitation the lion was also chasing me to kill for his prey, but when he chased me to a distance of about two miles I fell into the cow-men's hands who caught me at once as one of their cows which had been lost from them for a long time, then the lion got back from me at once for the fearful noise of these cow-men. After that they put me among their cows which were eating grass at that time. They thought I was one of their lost cows and put me among the cows as I was unable to change myself to a person again.

42

My Life with Cows

As I was among these cows I was illtreated as a wild or stubborn cow by these cow-men and always given double punishments which should only be given to the cows. At night they would put the whole of us in the yard and locked the door so that we might not escape. But as these cows were not persons and also more powerful, several times they would be scratching me with their horns and hoofs and jumping on me in the same place that I was cast down, and thinking that no doubt one day I should be killed or sold to a butcher who would kill me as an ordinary cow. The aim of these cows was to kick or scratch me with their horns until I would stand up and be doing as they themselves were doing. They were not sleeping, resting or tired of making fearful noises once till the day would break, especially if the rain comes at night and starts to beat us they would enjoy it to their satisfaction and then begin to kick themselves and dash at everything without mercy, because the yard was uncovered.

Every early morning the cow-men would come and take the whole of us to a wide pasture, and at the same time these cows would scatter on this pasture which was in the centre of the sun and start to eat the grasses voraciously, but I alone would cast myself down on the same place as I could not eat the grasses because I am not a real cow. Of course as a stream crossed the road on which we were travelling to this pasture so I was drinking the water from it when going early in the morning and also when returning in the evening and I was feeding only on this water as food. As I was unable to explain to these cow-men that I am not really a cow, so I was showing them in my attitude several times that I am a person, because whenever they were roasting yams in the fire and when eating it I would approach them and start to eat the crumbs of the yams which were falling down by mistake from their hands and whenever they were discussing some important matter with arguments within themselves I would be giving signs with my head which was showing them the right and wrong points on which they were arguing.

But one day, when they noticed that I was always standing or cast down in the same place and not eating the grasses or roaming about as other cows were doing, then they started to flog me with heavy clubs and also illtreat me as they were treating wild or stubborn cows, so I was feeling much pain and still I was unable to eat the grasses or to be doing as other cows were doing. Their aim was that if they flog me I would eat the grasses and do as other cows, but after they had tried all their efforts and failed then they thought that I was sick.

After the third day that they thought so, they took me to a market for sale, but unfortunately nobody bought me until the evening that the market closed, then they took me back home. Again, two days later they took me to this market for the second time for sale, but the butchers bought all the rest cows in the market and left me alone; everyone of them was telling these cow-men that if they take me back home they must kill me at once otherwise I would die unexpectedly. These butchers thought that I would die very soon as I could not do as other cows and also was very lean for want of food and again from illtreatment. So when these cow-men were returning to their town in the evening with me as no one bought me on that market day again, they were abusing and clubbing me repeatedly along the homeway. They were also thinking within themselves that if they take me to the market for the third time and if butchers refuse to buy me, then they would kill me unfailingly on that day for their food as I was not useful for them. But when the third market day arrived I was taken to the market for the third time, luckily I was bought by an old woman when it was about two o'clock p.m. The reason why she bought me was that her daughter's eyes were totally blinded for a long time and when she went to a fortune-teller, she was told that she must go to the market and buy a cow and kill it for a certain god which was in her town, then undoubtedly her daughter's eyes would see clearly as before. So when this old woman heard this from the fortune-teller then she came to the market and bought me very cheap as I was very lean, then she took me to her town where she would kill me for the god of her town as told.

When she reached her house, she tied me to a pillar which was on the front of her house, but this pillar was exposed to the sun or anything which might come down from the sky. Having tied me to this pillar she entered into the house and after half an hour she brought plenty of cooked yams back to me and I ate to my satisfaction as it was cooked. But when it was night she did not attempt to put me inside the house or a protected place for any dangerous creature which might attack me in the midnight. It was not yet eight o'clock in the night before everybody slept in this town, and again when it was ten o'clock a heavy rain came and beat me till the morning, and also the mosquitoes which were as big as flies did not let me rest once till the morning, but I had no hands to be driving them away from my body, although it is only in this "Bush of Ghosts" such big mosquitoes could be found, and as I was in the rain throughout the night I was feeling the cold so that I was shaking together with my voice, but had no fire to warm my body.

A Cola Saved Me

When it was twelve o'clock p.m. prompt the whole people of this town gathered at the front of the house of this old woman who bought me. After that four of them loosened me from the pillar and took me to their god which was outside the town. Having reached there I saw clearly that over fifty of these people held daggers or sharp knives, spears, cutlasses and axes which were as sharp as swords. The first ceremony which they performed for this god was that the whole of them laid me down flat and close before the god. At this stage I wanted to speak to them that I am not a real cow but a person. But all of this was in vain, because if my heart speaks as a person my mouth would speak out the words in the cow's voice which was fearful to them and also was not clear to them. As they laid me down before this god, all of them danced round me three times and this was the first ceremony to be performed. After that they were praying which was the second ceremony to be performed. But as the word "COLA" should be mentioned in a part of the prayer, and again the "COLA" should be produced at this point by the old woman as it must be included in this sacrifice before they could kill me before this god, so at this stage they asked the old woman to produce the "COLA". Then she searched her handbag which she

47

brought there, but when she searched the bag there was no "COLA", she had forgotten it at home, then she told them that she would run home and bring it.

But after she left a joke-man was joking funnily about me as I had become a laughing-stock for them, that he would eat cow meat today until he would nearly die, because he had eaten cow's meat for long time. And when a risible man who was among the four men who held me tightly before this god heard what the joke-man was saying then he started to laugh, so when the rest started to laugh together, the four men who held me before the god did not know the time that their hands slackened on me, then I sprang up unexpectedly with all my power to a distance of about ninety yards away. So this made them frightened as there were horns on my head, and before they could start to chase me I ran into a thick bush which was about a mile from them or that god. But after they tried all their efforts to catch me and failed, then the whole of them ran back to the town to take guns, bows and arrows. And before they could come back to chase me again, as I was running helter-skelter in that bush for my life I mistakenly fell into a very deep pond which was full of water as it was in the rainy season and also covered by the weeds which disallowed me from seeing that there was a pond. But to my surprise, immediately I saw my shadow in this water that I was a cow in form I changed to a person as before I used the smelling-ghost's juju which changed me so. Of course if I had known that if I see myself in water that I am a cow I would change to a person I should have done so immediately the cow-men caught me and before they sold me to the old woman whose daughter's eyes were blinded.

But as I had been changed to a person before these people came with guns, I asked them personally what they were looking for, but they replied that they were looking for a cow which was just escaped from them, then I said—"Oh! I saw it now when running far into the bush, better follow this way, you will see it very soon if you follow my advice." And the whole of them followed the direction that I showed them because they thought I was one of them. Then I left that area immediately they left me and I started to find the way to my home town.

But when it was about three months that I left them or changed from a cow to a person, one night, as I was wandering about in the bush I saw a dead wood which was about six feet long and three feet in diameter and there was a large hole inside it which was not through to the second end, which means it has only one entrance. So I entered the hole through this entrance, then I slept there as I did not sleep since I was among the cows before they sold me and again it was in the rainy season which was beating me about both day and night. But I did not wake until a "homeless-ghost" who was only wandering about since he was born by an unknown mother came and entered into the hole of this dead wood as he was also looking for such a dry place to sleep. But when he entered and met me there, he did nothing but got out cautiously and corked tightly the only entrance of this hole. After that he put it on his head while I was inside the hole, then he carried this wood about together with me, and he had carried it very far away before I woke inside this

49

wood as ghosts were very smart to trek either short or long distances.

But when I woke and noticed that I was carried away by an unknown ghost or creature to an unknown destination, so I began to suggest in my mind that perhaps the creature who is carrying me away now is going to throw the wood into a big fire or is going to throw it into a deep river. After I thought so, then I began to cry with a lower voice, not knowing that there was already a big snake inside this hole before I entered it. But at the same moment that the snake heard my voice when crying which was fearful to him, so he was coiled round me instead of running out of the hole as the entrance had been corked before by this "homeless-ghost" who was carrying it about. But as this snake was also fearful to me too, then I was crying louder than before, and when the "homeless-ghost" was hearing my voice inside this wood, it was a lofty music for him, then he started to dance the ghosts' dance and staggering here and there in the bush as if he was intoxicated by a kind of their drink which was the strongest of all their drinks and which was drunk only by "His Majesty" the king of the "Bush of Ghosts", the royal and prominent ghosts. The homeless-ghost who was carrying the wood away thought that it was this wood which he was carrying away that was playing the lofty music. But as he was carrying the wood away, dancing and staggering on, he met over a million "homeless-ghosts" of his kind who were listening to my cry as a radio. Whenever these ghosts met him and listened to my cry which was a lofty music for a few minutes, if they could not bear the music and stand still

าen the whole of them would start to dance at the same time as a madman. All these "homeless-ghosts" so appreciated my cry that all would dance to a distance of about a mile away from the carrier of the wood and then dance back to him again. And as all the ghosts that they met were joining them to dance, so all of them danced for three days and nights without eating, resting or being tired once until the news had spread to many towns of ghosts.

So at this time the homeless-ghost who was carrying the wood was invited by several prominent ghosts who had special occasions to perform. But whenever he reached the town that he was called to, first of all they would eat and drink to their most entire satisfaction, after that he would knock the wood as a sign, and when the snake heard it he would be running to and fro inside the wood in searching the way to go out and when doing that he would be also coiling me round in such a fearful way which would make me to cry more bitterly, and when hearing my cry then the whole of the ghosts of that town would be dancing till a late hour in the night as both day and night were the same for all ghosts.

But as a person could not cry from morning till the late hour in the night without stopping or eating once so if I stopped to rest for a moment or if my voice had become stiffness, then he would put this wood near the fire and if the wood started to heat, then I would start to cry louder by force, and the snake would be also dashing to every part of the hole as if ten persons are beating different kinds of drums to my cry, so they would continue at once to dance again.

51

At a Ghost Mother's
Birthday Function

As this "homeless-ghost" was then famous and well
known to every prominent ghost because of my cry
which was a very lofty music for them, so one day, a
famous ghost whose mother had died when all the eyes
of all the creatures were still on their knees invited all the
ghosts of his kind to his house as all the same kinds of
ghosts are living in the same town and called the homeless-
ghost to hear the music which would be the most important part for the ceremony of his mother's birthday.
But after all the invitees had gathered to his house, and
ate and drank to their satisfaction, then the homeless-
ghost knocked the wood as a sign, so I started to cry from
that morning till the evening, but as I never eat or drink
since the night he had corked me inside the hole, then
my voice was entirely stiffened or dead. I was unable to
cry any more, and as all these invitees had eaten and
drunk to excess, and still eager to hear my cry, so after
the whole of them with the "homeless-ghost" who carried
me to that town had tried all their efforts to make me cry
and failed, then he started to split the wood into two with
an axe. Luckily when the wood was half broken the

snake first found his way out as he was thinner than me and when visible to these ghosts unexpectedly all of them ran furiously to the house of the famous ghost who invited them and hid there. But as the wood had already nearly broken into two, so I tried my best and found my way out as well and without hesitation I ran into a far bush and hid there before they came back and it was already empty, so it was this time they knew that it was a person crying in it.

This is how I escaped from the "homeless-ghost" who was carrying me about, and before the dawn I had travelled very far away from that town and then entered into another town and started a new life with new ghosts. Immediately I entered this town I went round it and saw a ghost who only resembled earthly people among all ghosts who were living there. Then I entered his house, I saluted him with respect and he answered me exactly as an earthly person. He gave me a seat at once. After that I asked him to give me food as I did not eat anything since I escaped from the "homeless-ghost" who was carrying me about, but as he was a kind ghost he gave me the food without any question.

After I ate the food to my satisfaction and rested for some minutes, then I asked him whether he is an earthly person as I was doubting, he replied thus—"I am and I am not." But as I did not know which is to be held as the truth in these two answers, so I told him that I do not understand what he means by "I am and I am not." When heard so from me he started his story and also the story of that town as follows:

"You see, the whole of us in this town are burglars

and we have burgled uncountable earthly women in every earthly town, country and village. You earthly person, listen to me well, I shall tell you how we are burgling earthly women today. If an earthly woman conceives we would choose one of us to go to her at night and after the woman has slept then he would use his invisible power to change himself to the good baby that the woman would be delivered of whenever it is time. But after he has driven out the good baby and entered into the woman's womb, he would remain there and when it is time the woman would deliver him instead of the good baby which had been driven out; and the wonderful secret which all the earthly persons do not understand is that before two or three months that the woman bore him, he would develop rapidly as a year and an half old baby and would be very attractive to everyone, particularly the woman who bore him, as a good or superior baby. Having developed to that attractive state he would start to pretend to be sick continuously, but as he is very attractive to this woman, then she will be spending a lot of money on him to heal the sickness and also sacrificing to all kinds of gods. As this inferior baby has invisible power or supernatural power, so all the money spent on him and also the sacrifices would be his own and all would be stored into a secret place with the help of his invisible power.

But after the woman has spent all she has and become poor, then one night he would pretend as if he has died, so the woman who bore him as a superior baby, her family and other sympathisers would be saying thus: "Ah! that fine baby dies", but they do not know that he is not a superior baby. They would bury him as a dead baby, but the earthly persons do not know that he does not die but simply stops breath. But after he is buried, then he would come out of the grave at midnight, then he would go direct to the secret place where all the moneys and the sacrifices as sheep, goats, pigeons and fowls, all would be alive and are stored by his invisible power, and he would carry them to this town. So you earthly person, if you reach your earthly town and if you hear that a woman is delivering babies who die always or continuously, then believe, we are those babies and all the earthly people are calling such a baby "born and die". But if you do not believe this story if a "born and die" baby dies from a woman, after he is buried, watch the grave in which he is buried and after the second day try and go to that grave and dig it out; you would be very surprised that he would not be found there any more, but he has come back to this town. We have no other work to perform more than this in this town, so the whole of us in this town are called "Burglar-ghosts". But after he told me the story of their town and also about the "born and die babies" I was very impressed and surprised. He told me too that the whole of them are feeding on anything that earthly people have and said further that this is the meaning of "I am and I am not" when I first asked him whether he is an earthly person, because they were living as earthly persons and also as ghosts.

After he related the secret of the "born and die babies", then he asked me whether I should be living with him in that town and I said "yes", so he gave me a separate room in his house. But as I was living with this "burglar-ghost" and he was taking great care of me as if he was my father and mother, so one day, he told me that I should take care of everything in the house and said that he would go to a certain town which belongs to earthly people tonight, he said that he would return in ten months' time. Because he had told me before that he would try the wonderful invisible power once in my presence before I would leave him to believe all his saying. Of course as he told me like that I did not believe him at all and I did not know what he was going to do in that earthly town and also I did not know the name of the right earthly town he was going to. So when it was about one o'clock in the midnight he became invisible to me, because I did not see him walk out from the house on foot, so it remained me alone at home. But after he became invisible or gone away, I was playing about in this town as I could not stay at home always, but as it is not hard or very easy for a young boy to get a friend of his rank, by that I became a tight friend with a young ghost whose father was a rich ghost and also a native of that town when I was playing around the town. This young ghost taught me how to speak some simple ghosts' language. Of course I was unable to speak it fluently at that time. Both of us were playing about in the town in such a way that I did not remember to start to find the way to my home town again. But one night at about one o'clock in the midnight when I slept I heard somebody knocking the door of that house, when I opened this door which was a heavy flat stone it was this burglar-ghost who had gone ten months ago. Then he entered with bales of sewn clothes, sheep, goats, pigeons, fowls, all were still alive and moneys with all other used expensive articles.

At a Ghost Mother's Birthday Function

But when he loosened these bales of clothes there I saw plainly many clothes which belonged to my friends and my mother in my town that were among these clothes and was also surprised to see many clothes which my mother just bought for me and my brother before the war scattered all of us. After the second day that he came we killed all the fowls, pigeons, goats and sheep for the rest burglar-ghosts of this town for his good luck as he returned safely with many expensive articles. And when I saw all that he brought and also my own and my brother's properties, then I believed his story which he told me before he went away. Of course I could not ask him how he managed to get the clothes which belonged to me and my brother as I was too young to ask him such questions, so I left them for him and he sold all to another kind of ghosts who had no invisible power to do such work, but I ate those animals with them.

As I had already become tight friends with that young ghost before he returned from the earthly town, so one day this my young ghost friend told me to accompany him to his mother's town which was about twenty miles away from that burglar-ghosts' town, his mother was born and bred in this town which is the 8th town of ghosts. Having reached there his mother gave us food and drinks, and when we ate and drank to our satisfaction, then we were playing all about in the town with the other young ghosts of our ranks that we met there, but as we were playing about there I saw a very beautiful young ghostess, then I told my friend that I want to marry her, so my friend told her and also recommended me highly to her, so by that she agreed at the same time,

At a Ghost Mother's Birthday Function

but as her father was famous and prominent in that town, so he arranged the wedding day for the ghosts' next wedding day which was about nine days to come at that time as all the ghosts have a special day for marriage.

My First Wedding Day in the Bush of Ghosts

Before the wedding day was reached my friend had chosen one of the most fearful ghosts for me as my "best man" who was always speaking evil words, even he was punished in the fire of hell more than fifty years for these evil talks and cruelties, but was still growing rapidly in bad habits, then he was expelled from hell to the "Bush of Ghosts" to remain there until the judgement day as he was unable to change his evil habits at all. When the wedding day arrived all the ghosts and ghostesses of this town, together with the father of the lady whom I wanted to marry, my friend and his mother, my best man and myself went to the church at about ten o'clock, but it was the ghosts' clock said so. When we reached their church I saw that the Reverend who preached or performed the wedding ceremony was the "Devil". But as he was preaching he reached the point that I should tell them my name which is an earthly person's name and when they heard the name the whole of them in that church exclaimed at the same time— "Ah! you will be baptized in this church again before you will marry this lady."

When I heard so from them I agreed, not knowing that

My First Wedding Day in the Bush of Ghosts

Rev. Devil was going to baptize me with fire and hot water as they were baptizing for themselves there. When I was baptized on that day, I was crying loudly so that a person who is at a distance of two miles would not listen before hearing my voice, and within a few minutes every part of my body was scratched by this hot water and fire, but before Rev. Devil could finish the baptism I regretted it. Then I told him to let me go away from their church and I do not want to marry again, because I could not bear to be baptized with fire and hot water any longer, but when all of them heard so, they shouted, "Since you have entered this church you are to be baptized with fire and hot water before you will go out of the church, willing or not you ought to wait and complete the baptism." But when I heard so from them again, I exclaimed with a terrible voice that—"I will die in their church." So all of them exclaimed again that—"you may die if you like, nobody knows you here."

But as ghosts do not know the place or time which is possible to ask questions, so at this stage one of them got up from the seat and asked me—"by the way, how did you manage to enter into the 'Bush of Ghosts', the bush which is on the second side of the world between the heaven and earth and which is strictly banned to every earthly person to be entered, and again you have the privilege to marry in this bush as well?" So as these ghosts have no arrangements for anything at the right time and right place, then I answered that I was too young to know which is "bad" and "good" before I mistakenly entered this bush and since that time or year I am trying my best to find out the right way back to my

60

home town until I reached the town of "burglary-ghosts" from where I came with my friend to this town. After I explained as above, then the questioner stood up again and asked me whether I could show them my friend whom I followed to that town. Of course as my friend was faithful, before I could say anything, he and his mother whom we came to visit got up at the same time and said that I am living with a burglar-ghost in the town of the burglar-ghosts. But when my friend and his mother confirmed all that I said and as all the rest of the ghosts are respecting all the burglar-ghosts most because they were supplying them the earthly properties, so they overlooked my offence, then Rev. Devil continued the baptism with hot water and fire.

After the baptism, then the same Rev. Devil preached again for a few minutes, while "Traitor" read the lesson. All the members of this church were "evil-doers". They sang the song of evils with evils' melodious tune, then "Judas" closed the service.

Even "Evil of evils" who was the ruler of all the evils and who was always seeking evils about, evil-joking, evil-walking, evil-playing, evil-laughing, evil-talking, evil-dressing, evil-moving, worshipping evils in the church of evils and living in the evil-house with his evil family, everything he does is evil, attended the service too, but he was late before he arrived and when he shook hands with me on that day, I was shocked as if I touch a "live electric wire", but my friend was signalling to me with his eyes not to shake hands with him to avoid the shock but I did not understand.

Having finished the marriage service, all of us went

to my in-laws' house where everybody was served with a
variety of food and all kinds of ghosts' drinks. After that
all the ghost and ghostess dancers started to dance. Also
all the terrible-creatures sent their representatives as
"Skulls", "Long-white creatures", "Invincible and invisible Pawn" or "Give and take" who fought and won
the Red people in the Red-town for the "Palm-Wine
Drinker"; "Mountain-creatures", "Spirit of prey" whose
eye's flood of light suffocated Palm-Wine Drinker's wife
and also the "hungry-creature" who swallowed Palm-
Wine Drinker together with his wife when returning
from Deads'-town came and saluted my wife's father and
they were served immediately they arrived. But at last
"Skull" who came from "Skull family's town" reported
"Spirit of prey" to my wife's father who was chief
secretary to all the terrible and curious creatures in all
dangerous bushes, that the spirit of prey stole his meat
which the skull put at the edge of the plate in which both
were eating as both were served together with one plate,
because plates were not sufficient to serve each of them
with a plate. But before my wife's father who was their
chief secretary could have a chance to come and settle
the matter for them, both of them started to fight fiercely
so that all the ghosts and all the other representatives
came nearer and surrounded them, clapping hands on
them in such a way that if one of these fighters surrenders
or gives up it would be very shameful to him.

Some of these scene-lookers were clapping, and an old
Ape who was a slave and inherited by my wife's father
from his first generation since uncountable years was
beating a big tree under which both these terrible crea-

tures were fighting as a drum which had a very large
sound. But as this old slave ape was beating the tree as
a drum in such a way that all the scene-lookers who stood
round them could not bear the lofty sound of the tree
which was beaten as a drum and wait or stand still in
one place, so all the ghosts, evils, terrible creatures, my
friend, my wife and her father and myself started to
dance at the same time. But as I was intoxicated by the
strong drinks which I drank on that day, so I mistakenly
smashed a small ghost to death who came from the
"9th town of ghosts" to enjoy the merriment of the
marriage with us as I was staggering about.

At last I was summoned to the court of evil for wilfully
killing a small ghost, but as a little mistake is a serious
offence as well as big offence in the "Bush of Ghosts", so
the "Evil judge" judged the case at one o'clock of the
judgement day and luckily I was freed by a kind lawyer
whose mother was the native of the "Bottomless Ravine's
town", the town which belongs to only "triplet ghosts
and ghostesses". But if it was not far this incognito
lawyer who was very kind to me without knowing him
elsewhere I would be imprisoned for fifty years as this is
the shortest years for a slightest offence.

After I freed the case then I returned to my in-laws'
town and lived there with my wife for a period of about
three months and some days before I remembered my
mother and brother again, because I did not remember
them again when I married the lady. So one morning, I
told the father of my wife that I want to leave his town
for another one, but I did not tell him frankly that I want
to continue to find the way to my home town which I

left since I was seven years old. So I told him that I should leave with his daughter who was my wife, he allowed me to go or to leave, but disallowed his daughter to go with me. Of course, when I thought over within myself that however an earthly person might love ghosts, ghosts could not like him heartily in any respect, then I alone left his town in the evening after I went round the town and bade goodbye to the prominent ghosts.

On my Way to the
9th Town of Ghosts

As I left the town of my wife's father late in the evening, the town which is the 8th town of ghosts in which I was baptized with fire and hot water, so I travelled from bush to bush till a late hour in the night, perhaps I would see the way of my home town, but when I believed that I could not see it or I could not reach the 9th town of ghosts on that night, then I stopped under a tree and climbed to the top. I laid down on its branch which had plenty of leaves that covered me as a cloth from the cold of that night and also from the wind which was blowing the tree to and fro, with dew which was dropping as light rain on everything on the ground. But as I was troubled too much on the way to this tree by the ghost children, because I was very curious to them, so it was not more than five minutes before I fell asleep. And when it was about an hour and half that I was enjoying this sleep to my satisfaction, then I felt suddenly that somebody was knocking the tree at the bottom as if somebody is knocking a door, so I woke alert or with fear and when I bent downward and looked at the foot of this tree, there I saw a very short ghost who was not more than three feet high but very corpulent as a pregnant woman who would deliver either today or tomorrow. He was waving his hand to me to come down to him, but as I was looking at him all the while or for some minutes then I saw clearly that he had one arm, both his legs were twisted as rope and both feet faced sharply left and right, he had an eye on his forehead which was exactly like a moon, this eye was as big as a full moon and had a cover or socket which could be easily opening and closing at any time that he likes, no single hairs on his head and it was sparkling as polished ebony furniture.

When he noticed that I did not want to come down to him then he raised the cover of the eye off and at the same moment every part of this bush was as clear as daytime, and then I saw through this light that there were uncountable of the same kinds of these ghosts already surrounding the tree. All of them were waiting for me to come down to them, but as their attitude showed that they got ready to catch me, so by that I feared them.

But after they waited for a few minutes and believed that I stayed on this tree for their dreadful appearance then the whole of them came nearer to the tree and started to shake it with all their power, but when they nearly rooted out this tree then I fell on to their hands unexpectedly. I noticed carefully at this stage that if they are breathing in I would hear the cry of frogs, toads, pigs' cry, the crowing of cocks, the noises of birds and as if uncountable dogs are barking at the same time, and when they breathe out again there would be another cry of fearful creatures as well. But as the whole of them seized me by violence or rape at the same time, then I began to beg them with a lower or cool voice, because I thought that they were going to eat me alive and they did not listen to me until they took me to their town which is the 9th town of ghosts.

Having reached their town, they put me in a very dark room which was under the ground, as such rooms are very common in the "Bush of Ghosts". After a while they changed me to a blind man and then rubbed my body with their palms which were sharp as sand paper and were slightly scraping me as dulled sand paper. Having left that they were cutting the flesh of my body with their sharp finger-nails which were long at about four inches, so I was crying bitterly for much pain. Again after a little while they left that and then my eyes opened as before, but I saw nobody there with me in this doorless room who was ill-treating me like that. Immediately my eyes opened there I saw about a thousand snakes which almost covered me, although they did not attempt to bite me at all. It was in this doorless room which is in underground I first saw in my life that the biggest and longest among these snakes which was acting as a director for the rest vomited a kind of coloured lights from his mouth on to the floor of this room. These lights shone to every part of the room and also to my eyes, and after all of the snakes saw me clearly through the lights then they disappeared at once with the lights and then the room became dark as before.

After a few minutes later that these snakes disappeared, there I saw that this doorless room changed to a pitcher and unexpectedly I found myself inside this pitcher and at the same moment my neck was about three feet long and very thick, and again my head was so big so that my

67

long neck was unable to carry it upright as it was very stiff as a dried stick. Another two eyes which were as big and round as a football formed and appeared on this head and both eyes could be easily turning anywhere that I liked to look or see and I did not know where my normal eyes which were on my head before went. But as I was in this pitcher then all of these ghosts were visible to me and at the same time all were knocking the big head with sticks, but I had no hands to defend it because only my head and neck appeared out from the pitcher.

After some minutes they left knocking the big head, but I began to feel hunger as if I had not eaten anything for a year, so when I could not bear this hunger I started to cry out—"I want to eat." And immediately I was saying so there I saw on my front the food which I like most or which was exactly the same as the kind that my mother was always cooking for me in my town before we left. But as it was on my front my head could not reach it as my neck could not bend anywhere as a dried stick, of course when I tried my best and overturned the pitcher the head fell a little distance from this food instead of touching it, but as the neck was unable to bend or move the head, and the head was also too big for the neck to lift up, I tried all my power to touch the food more than thirty minutes before my mouth could reach the food and when I was about to start to eat it my mouth changed again to the beak of a small bird unexpectedly, but the food was still in front with its good flavour. When this beak disturbed me eating the food then I wanted to cry because I was feeling hunger as if I would die soon, but I cried out like a small bird instead of a man and when

68

all these ghosts that surrounded and looked at me as I was trying all the while to eat the food heard my cry as a small bird's cry all laughed at me at the same time.

So after I had tried all my efforts on everything and failed, then I was thinking in my mind that it is better for me to die now than to be in punishment like this, so immediately I finished these thoughts the beak disappeared together with the food and there was a mouth as usual and without hesitation I was moving together with the pitcher along the floor of this doorless room, but I saw nobody who was pushing me on and also all these ghosts which surrounded me disappeared unnoticed. At last I found myself where several roads meet together, the place was about one-third of a mile distant from their town, but all these roads were foot paths. After I moved to the centre of these roads by an invisible mover then I stopped. It was an open place, except the bush which spread on it. There I remained till the morning without seeing a single creature.

When it was about eight o'clock in the morning all the ghosts and ghostesses with their children of that town came to me with two sheep and two goats and also with some fowls. Having reached there the first thing they did was that the whole of them surrounded me, then all were singing, beating drums, clapping hands, ringing bells and dancing round me for a few minutes before they killed all the domestic animals which they brought before me and poured the blood of these animals on to my head which ran to the long neck and then into the pitcher in which the rest of my body was. After that the flesh of these animals was cooked and put all near to touch my mouth and I was easily eating it. So all these ghosts were coming every third day and worshipping me there as their god. But the worst part of it was the bells which they were beating with big rods whenever they came, and when sounding it would cause a head-ache, and again the blood of all the animals pouring on to my head was also smelling very bad when rotten. They were spending about four hours with me whenever they were coming to worship me, so I did not feel hunger again as I was eating all the sacrifices they were bringing to me.

Ah! nobody would enter into the "Bush of Ghosts" without much trouble and severe punishment, because as I was repeatedly beaten by rain and scourged by the sun on the centre of these roads as I was unable to move myself anywhere, so at night the bush animals, and other kinds of reptiles would come and stand before me and then looking at me with great surprise for my fearful appearance. And if all of them looked at me for so many hours, then the boa would come to me and start to swallow my head which appeared from the pitcher, but when it swallowed it to the larger part of the pitcher it would disturb him from swallowing the whole of me or the pitcher, and when disturbed then he would vomit me out again and I would not be allowed to sleep or rest for a minute throughout the nights because of the troubles given me by these animals. And if the day breaks again, all the sheep, goats, fowls, pigs and dogs would come again from that town. All would stand and look at me with much astonishment as I was curious and very dreadful to them, even to any person who might see me at this time. If these domestic animals look at me for some hours

70

attentively, motionless or crying once, then all the dogs who were among them would be barking at me and coming to me slowly until they would reach me and then they would start to eat the remaining sacrifice which I could not finish, and before they would finish that the goats and sheep would come to me and start to kick me on the head but I had no hands to drive them away. Again all these dogs would be licking all the blood poured on to my head with their tongues, and as they were doing like this all the ghosts would come again and then all these domestic animals would run back to the town, so by that I had no chance to sleep or rest both day and night.

Within a few months that I was at the centre of these roads in the pitcher news had reached every other town of ghosts of that area and all of them were trying their best to steal me for their towns as they thought that I am really a god.

River-Ghosts
Gala-day under the River

One night at about two o'clock, I saw many ghosts who came to me and put me inside a big bag which they brought. After that one of them put me on his head and then from there to their town which was under a big river, because they are "River-Ghosts". Which means they stole me from this centre of the roads to their town. Having reached their town they took me to their chief ancestor who sat down on an idle chair before a fearful god which they supposed to be the most powerful among their gods which they were worshipping in this town. Then they put me down before him as he was the one who ordered them to go and steal me from the centre of the roads when they heard information about me. Immediately I was presented to him he sent for a ram, then he killed it before me and poured its blood on to my big head which was as big as an elephant's head and also fearful to look at. After, they cooked the flesh of this ram and put the best fleshy parts of it before me to eat. But as I started to eat it the whole of them were very surprised and were also exceedingly glad as all their gods that I met there could not eat, breathe, or make any sign. But as these river ghosts or sceptical ghosts hate the heavenly God most and love earthly gods most, anything they wanted to do the chief ancestor would ask me first and if I made a sign with my head which would show him that the request should be done then he would tell the rest that I favoured them to do the requests, but if the sign showed that their requests should not be done then he would tell the rest that the requests are not granted by me, so therefore the requests would be cancelled at the same time. The chief ancestor was my interpreter as he only was permitted by his highest title to approach me at any time.

As I was so highly recognized by these river ghosts or sceptical ghosts so they built a one-roomed house and put me inside it and all of them were coming there to worship and sacrifice to me there as well. I was feeding on any sacrifice that I wanted and drinking the blood of the animals which they were killing and pouring on me as water, because they were not giving me water to drink. But as the blood was always pouring on me, so it was attracting flies which were covering me totally all the time and I had no hands to drive them away. Even sometime if the chief ancestor came in to visit me, he would not be able to discover me among these flies unless he first drove them away with a broom before he could see me.

When it was a week that they had brought me to their town the whole of them gathered together. First of all they opened the room in which they put me, after that the chief ancestor who only is permitted to approach me or to talk to me washed my head with my long stiff neck as only both appeared out from the pitcher, after this, he put a small red hand sewn cloth on the long neck which made it more ugly; after this, he put a kind of ghost's face cap on this my big head which made it more fearful to see. After that he put a kind of smoking pipe which was about six feet long into my mouth. This smoking pipe could contain half a ton of tobacco at a time, then he chose one ghost to be loading this pipe with tobacco whenever it discharged fire. When he lit the pipe with fire then the whole of the ghosts and ghostesses were dancing round me set by set. They were singing, clapping hands, ringing bells and their ancestral drummers were beating the drums in such a way that all the dancers were jumping up with gladness. But whenever the smoke of the pipe was rushing out from my mouth as if smoke is rushing from a big boiler, then all of them would laugh at me so that a person two miles away would hear them clearly, and whenever the tobacco inside the pipe is near to finish then the ghost who was chosen to be loading it would load it again with fresh tobacco as it was about three feet deep and four feet diameter.

After some hours that I was smoking this pipe I was intoxicated by the gas of the tobacco as if I drank much hard drink, because it was only ghosts could smoke such tobacco and it was only in the "Bush of Ghosts" such tobacco could be found.

So at this time I forgot all my sorrow and started to sing the earthly songs which sorrow prevented me from singing about since I entered this bush. But when all these ghosts were hearing the song, they were dancing from me to a distance of about five thousand feet and then dancing back to me again as they were much appreciating the song and also to hear my voice was curious to them. After a while all of them surrounded me closely, opened their mouths downward and looked at me with surprise. But as I was more intoxicated by the gas of the tobacco and also as the pipe was loaded continuously with fresh tobacco by the ghost who was specially chosen to be loading it, so by that I could not stop or tire of singing, and again my town's songs were then rushing to my heart at that time. So as they bent, their mouths which opened with great surprise downward onto my head the spit of these mouths was dropping on me and wet me as if I bathed with water, the spit was smelling so badly so that it was hard for me to breathe out or in.

After they listened to my songs for about half an hour, the chief ancestor took me out of this room which was specially built for me, then he rooted out a tall coconut tree which was about three hundred feet long, after that he put me on the top of this tree, then another ghost who was next in rank to him put the tree on his head upright which means I was on the topmost of it, after that he jumped together with the tree on to the chief ancestor's head so the chief ancestor, the one on his head who was next in rank to him, the tree and myself on this tree with all the rest ghosts and ghostesses were dancing together. But as I was intoxicated more and more by the gas of the tobacco which I was smoking in the pipe and also as the ghost who was loading it with fresh tobacco was so busy in loading it so that he could not see or talk to anybody at all at that time, so I was singing other earthly melodious songs which sorrow prevented me singing since

River-Ghosts. Gala-day under the River

I entered into this bush, in such a way that all the ghosts or every creature of this town were dancing, singing and shouting with joy and running warmly up and down in the town.

But as this "Gala-day" was so highly recognized with the new earthly songs which I was singing, so the King of the Bush of Ghosts whose seat is at the 20th town of ghosts, which is the capital for all the towns of ghosts sent an invisible message to the chief ancestor to bring me to him when he heard the information. But as the 20th town was very far away and again the invisible message was very urgent, so as all of these ghosts, together with the coconut tree were dancing up and down in the town as a crazy man, there I saw unexpectedly that one quill appeared on each side of the pitcher in which I was on the top of the coconut tree, after that one quill appeared on each side of the coconut tree as well, then ordinary feathers appeared on both arms of the ghosts, but the quills which appeared on the chief ancestor's arms were the largest and strongest because he would be the one who would carry the coconut tree together with me.

After that the whole of us flew by air to the 20th town the seat of H.M. the King of the Bush of Ghosts.

In the 20th Town of Ghosts

Within two hours in the air we reached the 20th town, but before we reached there millions of ghosts have been waiting and looking in the air for us. Immediately we appeared to them and they saw me at the front with the long pipe in my mouth with the smoke which was rushing out as from a big boiler, then the whole of them were shouting at me, pointing their hands at me and then rushing here and there to the King's palace. But when the palace could not contain all of them, then they rushed to their field which was about nine miles in diameter, then we landed on the centre of the field. It was very surprising to see over twenty thousand children smashed to death before we reached the field. Immediately we landed I started to sing and dance together with the tree, the ghost who carried the tree and the chief ancestor who carried us. When all the ghosts of this 20th town with H.M. the King could not bear to hear my earthly songs and also see my dance and sit down or to stand up motionless, then they joined us to dance, and again the smoke of the pipe was rushing out of my mouth continuously, because the ghost who was specially chosen to be loading it with the fresh tobacco did not neglect his duty at all.

In the 20th Town of Ghosts

But after the whole of them danced with me till the late hour in the night, then the chief ancestor commanded that the whole of us should stop and we did so but hardly as none of us were tired or satisfied. After that he commanded the coconut tree to stand still on the ground with a magical commandment, and at the same moment it stood on the ground as if it was planted there, then he commanded it again to bend down and it did so at once, after that he took me from the top of it and put me on the ground, again he commanded it to stand upright as it was and it did so.

They took me from this field to the palace. Having reached there they built a special doorless house which had only one room in this palace for me and put me inside it so that other kinds of ghosts might not steal me away before the day would break, because it was that day they specially arranged for "Gala-day" in the 20th town as the first one was a hint. After they put me inside this doorless house they also put uncut roasted sheep before me to eat, after that everyone went to his or her house to be preparing for tomorrow on which the "Gala-day" would be celebrated throughout.

Immediately they put this roasted sheep before me I was eating it greedily as I was very hungry in respect of the smoke of the tobacco which was intoxicating me like hard drink. But as I was eating it greedily and when it was one o'clock midnight the wall of this house split into two suddenly and there I saw another kind of ghost enter through that space. I looked at him with fear as he was not a native of the 20th town, then he came to me cautiously with a big coil of rags of cloth on his head.

The first thing he did, he sat down and started to eat the meat and within a minute he finished it. For this reason I was so frightened and also his exceedingly fearful appearance with his harmful attitude, so I tried to run away but the pitcher did not allow me at all.

Having finished the meat, without hesitation he put me on his head, he got out of the palace cautiously and then kept going in the town to an unknown place. But as this 20th town is a large town he travelled for about two hours before he reached the gate of the town. As the gate is watched both day and night so he met the gate-keeper at the gate. When the gate-keeper saw me on his head he challenged him that where he was carrying me to, but instead of answering the gate-keeper's question he was only telling him to open the gate for him to pass. But when the gate-keeper insisted and after both argued for a few minutes, then he put me down closely to him, after that both were fighting fiercely so that all the other creatures who were living at the back of the gate woke up from sleep and came nearer to the scene, they were looking and laughing at them, as the gate-keeper was struggling to take me from him and return me to the palace and the ghost who was carrying me away was also struggling violently to take me away to his town.

After they were fighting fiercely for about two hours so as the gate-keeper has seven of the same kind of juju which he could use to change the night to day seven times, because he has no power at night but only in the day, and again the ghost who was taking me away has eight jujus which could change the day to the night as well because he has no power in the day, so the gate-keeper first threw down one of his seven jujus on the ground and at the same moment night changed to the day, so he become more powerful than the one who was carrying me away as he has no power in the day. Then he too threw one of his eight jujus on the ground and that day became night at once and then he became more powerful than the gate-keeper. Both of them were using their juju like this until the gate-keeper had used all his own, but the ghost who was carrying me away still had one. At last he used the one which still remained with him, it changed that day to the night at the same time, so he had more power, then he started to fight the gate-keeper who had been already powerless. But as the gate-keeper received heavy blows from him, so he fell down suddenly, but the ghost who carried me to that place laid down on the gate-keeper and beat him greedily. So the ghost who carried me to that gate kicked the pitcher in which I was unnoticed and it broke into pieces, so immediately my body touched the ground then I changed at once to my former form before they put me in the pitcher. But as both of them were still fighting fiercely and did not know that the pitcher had been broken and I have come out of it, so without hesitation I took to my heels and left them there.

Immediately I came out from the pitcher, and then running away in the bush at that night uncountable flies which were following me along nearly made me suspected, because all the blood of all the animals which were poured on me as sacrifice was rotten on my body as black paint and was smelling so bad so that it collected these flies from the hidden place that they slept, even the

80

cloth which my mother wove for me before I entered this Bush of Ghosts had torn into rags by the rotten blood.

Of course as I did not stop once so I ran far away from that gate before the dawn so that I might not be recaptured by the ghosts of the 20th town. When it was dawn I stopped and rested for some hours. After that I started to wander about searching for the way to my home town as usual. But as I was wandering about in this bush I saw a dead animal's skin which had been killed for long time by an unknown creature, so I took its skin and still went on, because it was very stiff to wear at that time. A few hours later I travelled to a pond, the water of this pond was as clean as if it was filtering every hour, it was under a bush which was not thick but big trees covered it like a roof and prevented the sun shining on it, so by that its water was always as cool as ice. I met many pieces of the ghost's soap at the bank nearly falling inside the water, so this showed me that the users of this pond were not so far from that place.

Immediately I discovered it, first I listened attentively for some minutes perhaps I would hear the noises of the creatures or ghosts who might be coming to draw water at that time or perhaps a town of ghosts would be near there, but when there was no noise or voice of any creature heard, even a bird did not cry near that place at all, then I put the skin down at the bank and entered this pond. I drank the water to my satisfaction as I never tasted either fresh or dirty water since I was in the pitcher, except the blood of the animals poured on me as sacrifice with the spit of their mouths which was dropping on to my head when opening them and looking at me with much surprise as I was singing the earthly songs which were newly born into the town of the aquatic ghosts and also in the 20th town which is the capital.

After that I washed away the rotten blood off my body, then I washed the skin of the animal as a cloth, after that I looked round this pond and saw a place where the sun reached the ground, so I went there and spread this skin there to dry, having done that I went to a thick bush which was as a roof, I hid under it and hastily looked at my back, my front, my left and right and also up and down with a doubtful mind perhaps a ghost or a harmful creature might be coming at that time to catch me.

But as the bush which surrounded this pond was very quiet without any noise of a creature whatever it might be so I began to feel much cold without being cold, and when my heart was not at rest for the quietness of that place then I went to the place that I spread the skin in the sun and began to warm myself in this sun perhaps my body would be at rest, but when there was no change at all until the skin was dried then I took it and left that area as quickly as possible. So I wore it as a cloth, of course, it could only reach from my knees to the waist, so I was going on with it like that. It was on this day I believed that if there is no noise of a creature in a bush or if a bush is too quiet there would be fear without seeing a fearful creature.

After I had travelled to a short distance from the pond I stopped under a tree as it was then in the evening, then I started to think what I could eat because there was nothing more edible than the small fruits which had fallen down from this tree where I sat at its foot, although I did not know the name of the fruits or its tree as they belonged only to ghosts of that area. When I tasted them, they were very sour, though I ate them like that as there was no other food or any edible thing there for me again. Having finished these fruits at about eight o'clock I was looking for a safe place to sleep. After a few minutes I saw a large tree which was near that place and there was a huge hole in its body which could contain a person. Not knowing that this hole was the home of an armless ghost who had been expelled from his town which belonged only to all the armless ghosts. When I entered this hole I travelled to a part of it which contained me, but it still went further, so I laid down and fell asleep at the same time, because I had no chance to sleep or rest once for all the time that I spent inside that pitcher. But when it was about twelve o'clock in the midnight this armless ghost who was the owner of the hole wanted to go out, of course, I did not know that somebody was living there before I entered.

As he could only go out at night to fetch his food, so when he reached the place that I slept he stumbled on me and fell down unexpectedly, because he did not know that somebody was there already and also the hole was very dark, so some part of his body was wounded as he was armless to defend himself. I woke up unexpectedly as he fell down on me suddenly, after a few minutes he tried his best and got up with pain, then he asked with rage—"Who is that?" Of course, as my friend the young ghost in the town of the ghost burglars had taught me some of the ghosts' language, so I replied—"I am an earthly person."

But when he heard the words of "earthly person" from me, he exclaimed—"Oh you are the one who is always coming here and stealing all my property whenever I go out, I will catch you this night, just hold on for a minute." Having said so he cried out louder to the other ghosts who are his partners to come and help him to grip me as he is armless. But before his partners could reach there I jumped down from the hole to the outside, and without any ado I started to run away that night for my life. Immediately I jumped down and ran away I met over one thousand ghosts who were rushing to his hole to help him, but at the same time that they met me all of them did not go to him direct to hear what he called for, instead of that all were chasing me as I was running away as fast as I could. When they chased me to a short distance to catch me and failed then they got back from me to the armless ghost to hear what he called them for. But I was still running away, I did not stop, as I thought within myself that perhaps if I stop to rest for a few minutes they might come again to catch me, so by that I was still running away faster until I stepped into a part of the ground of this bush. But to my surprise at the same moment that I put my left foot on it to be still running away it was saying thus with a loud voice—"Don't smash me! oh don't smash me, don't walk on me, go back to those who are chasing you to kill you, it is paining me too much as you are smashing me."

When I heard this so suddenly, I was so frightened so that I withdrew my foot back at once and I heard no

84

voice again. After that I turned to another part and smashed it with the same foot as well, perhaps that part would not cry out—"don't smash me." But I heard the same caution suddenly with louder voice, so I withdrew my foot from it, then I stopped there and asked myself this question—"can land talk like a human being, or can land feel pain if somebody smashes it?" After I asked myself this question with a dead voice, as there was nobody to ask and explain it to me, so I turned back at once to look for where is possible to travel or run in this bush without any noise, but I saw more than one thousand of the armless ghost's partners that were hunting for me up and down in this bush to catch me and kill me, after they heard from the armless ghost what I had done to him. When they nearly traced me out and I believed that if they caught me no doubt they would kill me instantaneously, so without hesitation I jumped onto this "talking-land", running away as fast as I could. Then it started to speak as before, of course, I did not listen to what it was saying, I was only running on faster to leave that "talking-area" in time to the "talkless-area" to hide myself in a safe "talkless-place", because this "talking-land" was showing the place that I was reaching in the bush to these ghosts. But as I was still running on fiercely and with fear I did not know the time I mistakenly entered into another bush which was more dreadful than the "talking-land".

Immediately I entered it every part of it was blowing alarm, which was very fearful to hear and remain there, because it was blowing as if enemies are approaching a town. Then I stopped suddenly behind a tree as the noises of these alarms were so curious and too fearful for me. To my surprise immediately I stopped all the alarms stopped blowing at once, but there I saw a very young ghostess who hid herself under a small bush which covered the bottom of this tree. She ran out unexpectedly and when she ran out I saw her clearly that she was very ugly so that she could not live in any town of ghosts, except to be hiding herself about in the bush both day and night for her ugly appearance. But her ugly appearance was so curious to me that I was chasing her as she was running away to see her ugliness clearly to my satisfaction, because I had never seen such a very ugly creature as this since I was born and since entered the Bush of Ghosts.

Again, at the same moment that I left the place that I stood behind this tree the alarms started to blow according to how I was chasing this ugly ghostess and I was unable to stop in one place so that the alarms might stop, my aim was only to see the ugliness of this ugly ghostess clearly, because as she was running away so that I might not see her ugliness it was so she was laughing louder at her ugliness and I was also laughing louder at the ugliness. As I was chasing her to and fro to look at her ugliness it was so this bush was blowing various fearful alarms and this was pointing out how I was running and how far reaching in the bush to the ghosts who were chasing me at the back to kill me. This young ghostess was so ugly that if she hid under a bush and if she looked at her ugly body she would burst suddenly into a great laugh which would last more than one hour and this was detecting her out of the hidden place she might hide herself. She could not live with any ghost or other kind of creature because of her ugly appearance. As I was chasing her fiercely to and fro for a long time it was so those ghosts who were chasing me to kill me were approaching nearer, because these alarms were blowing repeatedly and showing what I was doing. This ugly ghostess did not allow me to look at her ugliness as she was running and laughing with all her power and full speed until I was seeing all these ghosts slightly and they were also seeing me slightly before I hid behind a tree, but at the same moment that I stood on a place it was so all these alarms stopped blowing, which means this bush wanted me to be in one place until these ghosts would come and kill me there.

Having rested for a few minutes then I remembered again the ugliness of this ugly ghostess, but at that time I was seeing these ghosts clearly and they were also seeing me clearly. But as I determined to see or to look at the ugliness of this ghostess to my satisfaction and said— "It is better for me to die than to leave this ugly ghostess and run away without seeing her ugliness clearly to my entire satisfaction.

"This will be a great surprise to everybody to hear that I see something which is more interesting for me than the 'death' which is coming behind to kill me."

Immediately I remembered her ugliness again I started to chase her on, because I did not care for any consequence at that moment at all. But as these ghosts were near to catch me before I started to chase the ugly ghostess for the second time and again these alarms were then blowing with another terrible sound, so I could not

87

chase her so far before the hands of these ghosts were touching me at the back and slightly to grip me. When I believed that this ugly ghostess would not wait or stop for me in a place to look at her ugly appearance to my satisfaction then I branched from her and started to run to another part of this bush.

In the Spider's Web Bush

As these ghosts did not stop in chasing me along so after I ran further in this "alarm-bush" there I saw a bush which was almost covered with spiders' webs in front at a distance of about eighty yards, then I pretended to stop and not to run to it, but when these ghosts nearly gripped me I ran to this "spider web bush" unnoticed, of course they were banned from entering it. And after I ran to a distance of seven feet in this "spider web bush" and when I was stopped from running along by this thick web, so I turned sharply at once back to come out of it, and instead of coming out easily I was simply wrapped as a chrysalis by the web, at the same time I was held up by it and dangled to and fro by the breeze as a dried leaf. Immediately I was held up and dangling all these ghosts went back as they were strictly banned from entering it, because it belonged only to a kind of ghosts who are "spider eating ghosts". This "spider web bush" was totally covered with spiders' web as a fog in a season. There was no single tree, bush, refuse, or plants which are usually found in other bushes, but only the spiders and their web represented them. The town of these "spider eating ghosts" is separated from all other kinds of ghosts. They were fond of eating spiders which were the most important food for them, so therefore no other kinds of ghosts should enter there. I was so wrapped that I was hardly able to breathe out easily, even it so straightened me that I could not bend anywhere as a dried stick and I could not cry out for help, because it corked my mouth as a bottle and I could not see anywhere whether any danger or harmful creature was coming there to kill me.

So I remained there helplessly, except the breeze or wind which was blowing me to and fro. When it was about seven hours that I was wrapped and held up there a heavy rain came, beating me till the third day that one of the "spider eating ghosts" came to eat the spiders. This rain beat me so that the web which wrapped me tightly soaked my body as if I was bathed with water. As he came to eat the spiders on this day and as he was going round there searching for the spider and when he saw me dangling to and fro he stopped suddenly at a little distance from me and looking at me for some minutes before he came to me then he pressed every part of my body with his hands, although I did not see him with my eyes but was hearing his foot noise and also feeling on my body that he was pressing it with his hands. Having pressed it for a few minutes then he was saying thus—"Oh! I thank God almighty today, I discover my father whom I had been looking for, many years ago, and I do not know that it is here he died when he came to eat the spiders so I shall take him to the town for burial and the other ceremony. Ah! I thank God today." He was exceedingly glad as he discovered me as the dead body of his father, then he took me on his head and kept going to the town at once with joy, he did not wait and eat the spiders on this day at all.

In the Spider's Web Bush

When he carried me and appeared in the town all his town's ghosts asked him that what sort of heavy load he was carrying and sweating as if he bathed in water like this, so he replied that it was the dead body of his father who died in the "spider web bush" when he went there to eat the spiders. But when his town's ghosts and ghostesses heard so, they were shouting with joy and following him to his house. Having reached his house and when his family saw me how I swelled up as a pregnant woman who would deliver either today or tomorrow they thought that it was true I was the dead body of their father, so they performed the ceremony which is to be performed for deads at once. After that all the ghosts of this town were dancing the native dance of the "spider eating ghosts" round me, because all the rest of the ghosts of this town also thought I am his father and again this father could eat spiders more than the rest.

Then they told a ghost who is a carpenter among them to make a solid coffin. Within an hour he brought it, but when I heard about the coffin it was at that time I believed that they wanted to bury me alive, then I was trying my best to tell them that I am not his dead father, but I was unable to talk at all as the web corked my mouth hard and I was unable to shake my body to show them that I am still alive, it was in vain. So after the carpenter brought the coffin, then they put me inside it and also put more spiders inside it before they sealed it at once, they said that I would be eating the spiders which they put inside this coffin along the heaven's road, because they thought that if somebody died he would be eating along the heaven's road before he would reach heaven. After that they dug a deep hole as a grave in the back yard and buried me there as a dead man.

As I was inside this grave in the coffin I was thinking within myself that—"Can I be saved from this grave or is there anybody to save me out of this?" then I said—"I shall put hope on God that He shall save me out of the coffin and out of the grave." But luckily at last my thoughts became the truth, so when it was one o'clock in the midnight a resurrectionist who was present when they buried me there came and dug out the coffin, then he broke it and took me out of it. He put me on his head and kept going to another far bush again. His aim was to eat the spiders which were on the web that wrapped me and also to eat me. As he stole me from the grave and went hastily along in the bush that night he was meeting several ghosts of his kind in the bush, and whenever they met him and asked what he carried like this, he would answer that it is the dead body of his father who died yesterday. He would tell them further that he is going to bury him very far into the bush so that he might not be smelling to anybody in the town when decayed. He would not tell them the truth that he stole me from the grave and he is going to eat me. Whenever he was explaining to them like this they would be sorry for him and then he kept going on his way. It was that night I believed that thieves are giving themselves much severe punishment whenever they steal important things, because as he was talking to those whom he was meeting on the way his voice was trembling with fear and his body was also shaking and looking here and there perhaps somebody was chasing him to catch the thief of the dead body, he was unable to wait and attend to them satisfactorily before he would leave them unnoticed and keep going.

As he was going hastily zigzag in the bush it was so he was dashing at both trees and hills and always mistakenly falling into the deep holes, and several times he would jump on thorns unnoticed, but he would not be able to wait and take care of himself, as he was thinking that they were chasing him from the town to catch as a thief. Having gone very far into the bush he reached a place which was cleared some time ago by an unknown creature, then he put me down and without hesitation he gathered some dried sticks and prepared the fire in which he would roast me and eat me as meat. But immediately he put me inside this fire the spider web which wrapped me could not catch fire as it was very wet from the rains which were beating me repeatedly in the "spider web bush" before I was taken to the town for burial. Again the fire was insufficient to burn the web away from my body before I could be roasted, because the dried sticks were very scarce near there. But at the same time that he put me on this fire about twelve ghosts of his kind appeared and came to him, then they asked him what he wanted to do in that place. He replied that it was the dead body of a "spider eating" ghost's father, he stole from the grave to roast and eat. But as all these ghosts heard so from him they were jumping up with gladness, they told him that they would eat me with him. He was very annoyed when he heard so, as he alone wanted to eat me.

As the fire which had been prepared before these

ghosts appeared to him was insufficient to roast me and luckily as the dried sticks were very scarce to get near there, so he sent two of these ghosts to go for the dried sticks, but these two selected ghosts refused totally to go, unless the whole of them would go, because they were thinking that it was a trick, so the rest would eat me before they would come back when fetching the dried sticks. When these two selected ghosts refused to go unless the whole of them would go together, then he told them to go together, but the whole of them said again unless he would follow them as well before they would go. After they argued for some minutes then all of them together with the one who brought me there went to fetch the dried sticks. But after they went away and left me there and as this fire was yet half quenched, so I tried my best and laid my body on it. After some minutes the web became half-dried and caught the fire which was slowly burning the web, then I found my way out by force from the web, of course, it burnt some parts of my body slightly. Without any ado I took to my heels and before they could return from the place that they went for the sticks I had gone very far into another bush which did not belong to them. This is how I was saved from the spider-eating ghosts who buried me alive. Immediately I escaped then I travelled to the south-east of this bush perhaps I would see the way to my town and perhaps I might see something to eat as I was feeling hunger.

At that moment a heavy rain with a very strong wind came. This wind was blowing here and there so that many trees were falling down unexpectedly, so I stopped and looked for a safe place to shelter myself from the rain and to save my life from all the trees which were falling down here and there by the strong wind. But as I was looking for such a place there I discovered a place which was close to a big tree with props and I thought that the place was refuse of dried leaves which were heaped together closely to this tree, because it was so dark at that time so that I could not see everything clearly, even I could not see myself as well. So I laid down and crept into it, not knowing that it was inside the pouch of a kind of the animal who has a big pouch or bag under his belly, I entered as he had already sheltered himself there before me. So I simply entered it. But as it was warm slightly like a room I fell asleep in it within a minute. But when the rain with the strong wind were too heavy or too much for him to bear and remain there, he left that place and looked about for another place to shelter himself, and did not discover such a place until he reached a bush which belongs to the 13th town, which only belongs to short ghosts, but I did not wake at all in his pouch as he was carrying me about until he reached this bush.

The Short Ghosts and their Flash-eyed Mother

As all the short ghosts of this 13th town were not doing other work more than to go to bush to hunt for bush animals, to kill them and to bring them to the "flash-eyed mother" who is their ruler, so this animal fell into their hands at about nine o'clock in the morning. They shot him to death at once with guns, after that all of them started to drag him to their town as he was too heavy for them to carry on their heads. But I did not wake as they were doing all these things. Having reached the town, all the rest of the short ghosts of this town gathered together round this curious animal. All were looking at him with much surprise as this kind of animal was so scarce to get or see frequently in their bush. But as the hair on his body should be first scraped off carefully and kept in a safe place, as it is very precious to all of them, so at first they scraped the hair on the first part of his body and when they were scraping the hair inside the pouch in which I slept, so the scrapers or knives which they were using mistakenly touched one of my feet suddenly, then I woke inside the pouch, but as I shook my body to left and right to come out as I did not know that it was inside the pouch of an animal I slept, I thought

96

The Short Ghosts and their Flash-eyed Mother

I was inside a room. So as I shook, the pouch shook as well in their view and immediately all of them took their guns ready to shoot the pouch; they thought that the animal became alive again. But as one of them was wiser, he noticed carefully that only the inside or a part of the pouch was shaking, then he expanded it and saw me there. Having discovered me he held both my feet and dragged me out unexpectedly and I simply found myself in the centre of them.

The first thing I did immediately I got out was to run away to save my life, but I was not allowed. All of them were looking at me with their terrible eyes for about half an hour. They did not talk or shake their bodies as a dummy. As they were too terrible for me to look at or to stand with, then I was running away for the second time, perhaps I would be safe from them. But all of them gripped me violently and took me before an old woman who is the "flash-eyed mother" the ruler of that 13th town and she was the only woman in this town. As I stood before her on this critical day and when I saw her clearly, I closed my eyes tightly at the same moment, I could not open it till I was forced to open it by these short ghosts who escorted me before her and still I was unable to open it in full, because of her fearful, dreadful, terrible, curious, wonderful and dirty appearance.

This "flash-eyed mother" sat on the ground in the centre of the town permanently. She did not stand up or move to anywhere at all, she was all the time beaten there by both rain and sun, both day and night. There was no single house built in this town as she alone filled the town as a round vast hill, it was hard for the rest inhabitants to move about or to sleep in the town. This town is about six miles in circumference, it was as clean as a football field. All these short ghosts were just exactly a year and an half old babies, but very strong as iron and clever while doing everything, all of them had no other work more than to be killing the bush animals with short guns like pistols which were given to them by the "flash-eyed mother" and whenever an animal is killed they would bring it to her in the same place that she sat. Millions of heads which were just like a baby's head appeared on her body, all circulated set by set. Each of these heads had two very short hands which were used to hold their food or anything that they want to take, each of them had two eyes which were shining both day and night like fire-flies, one small mouth with numerous sharp teeth, the head was full of long dirty hair, two small ears like a rat's ears appeared on each side of the head. If they are talking, their voices would be sounding as if somebody strikes an iron or the church bell which sound would last more than ten minutes before stopping. If all of them are talking together at a time it would be as a big market's noises, they were arguing, flogging and reporting themselves to their mother. They could not move about or from the body of their mother to another place. Their mother had a special long and huge head which she was using to talk and to feed herself, it was above everything in the town and it showed her out from a distance of about four miles from this town. She had a large mouth which could swallow an elephant uncut. The two fearful large eyes which were on the front of her head were always flashing or bringing out fire

The Short Ghosts and their Flash-eyed Mother

whenever she was opening them, and this is why all the rest ghosts and ghostesses with all other creatures gave her the name of "flash-eyed mother". There were over a thousand thick teeth in this mouth, each was about two feet long and brown in colour, both upper and lower lips were unable to cover the teeth. The hair on her head was just as bush, all could weigh more than a ton if cut and put on a scale, each was thicker than a quarter of an inch and almost covered her head, except the face. All these hairs were giving shelter to her whenever it was raining and whenever the sun was scorching her as she was not walking to anywhere. Both her hands were used in stirring soup on the fire like spoons as she did not feel the pain of fire or heat, her finger nails were just like shovels and she had two very short feet under her body, she sat on them as a stool, these feet were as thick as a pillar. She never bathed at all.

It was these eyes which were bringing out splashes of fire all the time and were used to bring out fire on the firewood whenever she wanted to cook food and the flash of fire of these eyes was so strong that it would catch the firewood at the same moment like petrol or other inflammable spirit or gunpowder, and also use it at night as a flood of light in lighting the whole town as electricity lights, so by that, they were not using other lights except the flash fire of her eyes. Whenever one or more of the short ghosts who were serving her as their mother offended her, both eyes would be flashing out fire on to the body who offends her, and the fire would be burning the body at the same moment as fluffy things or rags. She was using it as a whip to flog any other of her offenders as

99

it could be flashed to a long distance. For this reason she was very fearful to other creatures coming to her town without special reason, even H.M. the King of the Bush of Ghosts could not say—"Who is she?" She was using all kinds of animal skins as clothes which made her more fearful, ugly and dreadful to see or look at. As she was not standing up or moving about so all the short ghosts of this town who were under her flag were killing the bush animals and bringing them to her, although all of them were feeding on these animals as well.

I was escorted before her on this day and stood before her as if I had been dissolved into vapour or no more alive and also dreaming of her terrible, dreadful, ugly, dirty appearance without sleeping. She asked the short ghosts whether I am the son of the animal from whose pouch they took me out, all of them replied that they could not say definitely. After she heard so from them, then she flashed the fire of both her eyes on to my body and it burnt the animal skin which I wore as a cloth and also burnt some part of my body as well at the same time, because she wanted to know whether I could talk or not, but as my body caught fire and I cried suddenly with a loud voice, so when they heard my sorrowful voice the whole of them burst into a great laugh at a time as if uncountable cannons fired together, and her own laugh among the rest was just as if a bomb explodes, and as her own voice was louder in a very queer way, terrible and dreadful, so some of the big trees on hills around this town fell down, and I myself nearly sank into the ground to half of my body before some of these short ghosts pulled me out of the ground. But after she heard my

100

voice she believed that I am an earthly person, but she did not know how I managed to be in the Bush of Ghosts.

Having believed that I am an earthly person then she asked me whether I would live with her, so I replied—"yes". But she did not ask whether I escaped from somewhere or offended somebody before I reached there. After I agreed to her request she ordered the short ghosts to give me a short gun to be hunting with them. These short ghost hunters taught me how to kill the bush animals. Having qualified as a hunter, then I followed them to the bush. Whenever we were killing an animal we would bring it to "flash-eyed mother" who was supposed to be our mother or guardian, so she would take it from us and cook it at the same time in the same place that she sat permanently like a stump. Having cooked it, the first thing she was doing was to serve the fleshy part of the animal to all the heads that surrounded her body, after that she would serve the rest fleshy part to herself and then the bony part to all the short ghosts. If all the heads and herself were eating at the same time their mouths would be making noises as if one hundred winches are working together. Within a minute all the heads would finish their own, then would be asking for more immediately as they were not satisfied with small food, so for this reason the mother was not serving us with enough food so that it might be sufficient for them. All of them would be fighting, arguing and flogging themselves while eating the food greedily and also the biggest head which belongs to their mother would be settling their misunderstandings for them several times before they would finish the food. As she added the dirt as her beauty, so she was not checking all the heads from passing urine, excreta and spitting on her body which would wet all over her body.

One day when we went to the bush since morning it was hard for us before we killed a very small animal at about 4.30 p.m., then we brought it to her. Having cooked it, she served very little to every one of the heads in such a way that the remainder would reach every one of us, but all these heads protested because the "flash-eyed mother" served us out of it, they wanted to eat all, of course when their mother noticed that they protested she took all that she served to every one of us back from us and then shared it for them, because she did not want them to be hungry at any time, so all of us slept that night with empty stomachs. But when it was early in the morning all of us struck going to the bush to hunt. When she noticed that we struck she called the whole of us before her, she asked us to bring the animal which we killed for food that morning, but we said none, we told her further that we did not go to bush at all that day. Immediately she heard so from us, she was exceedingly annoyed and started to flash the fire of her eyes on to us with all her power, so that the skins of the animals that every one of us wore caught fire at once as by petrol and this means she was flogging us. As she was flogging us with the fire all the heads on her body were also abusing, scorning and cursing us badly.

After that she ordered us to go to bush at once and we must not come back without an animal, otherwise all of us would be burnt to ashes willing or not, she concluded. Then all of us went to the bush at the same time. Having

102

reached the bush God is so good, within an hour we killed a kind of ghosts' animal which had plenty of fat like a pig, then we brought it to her. Having cooked it she served all the heads to their entire satisfaction, after that she served herself to her satisfaction and then served us last according to the rule and regulation given to her by the heads. So the whole of us ate this animal to our entire satisfaction, because this animal was as big as an elephant and also fatty.

She had a kind of a terrible alarm which was in a hidden part of her body, but it was not visible to us, except those heads and herself. It was this alarm she was blowing every early in the morning to wake us up, but it would be after she had cooked a kind of short ghosts' pap before it would be blowing repeatedly with a terrible sound. Whenever we heard it, every one of us would be in a single line before her as soldiers and as every one of us had his own small basin or cup which were made by them, then she would be serving us one by one with the pap which would be poured into the cups; it would reach the half. It was like this we were receiving it as when soldiers are receiving their rations before an officer and all the heads had their own cups as well, but all the times that their mother was serving us all of them would be telling her seriously and repeatedly that she was serving us with much food. These heads were always making noises and all of them were not sleeping at the same time at night, because if some of them sleep, the rest would be talking until those who were sleeping would wake. Some times they would be abusing their mother whenever she was sleeping and also snoring or snorting as if a sea is

The Short Ghosts and their Flash-eyed Mother

roaring with great power as follows:— "Hear our 'flash-eyed mother' who is snoring like strong wind." But if she woke at that moment they would tell her with louder voice—"Take away your flash eyes from us."

Barbing Day in the Town of Short Ghosts

As all the heads which were on the body of "flash-eyed mother" and also all short ghosts' heads were full of much thick and dirty hair like weeds, so they were only barbing once in a century when the "Secret Society of Ghosts" festival is near.

So that a special full day is reserved for barbing their heads and their barber is one of the "fire creatures" who was qualified for barbing heads with the clippers and knife of fire. But when it was announced by the "flash-eyed mother" that the barbing day would be tomorrow I thought our heads would be barbed with the ordinary clippers, scissors and knives as in my home town, so I was jumping up with gladness because I was never barbed once since about fourteen years that I entered the Bush of Ghosts. So when the day was reached all of us were bound to be in one spot. After a few minutes there I saw a creature who was fire and held the clippers of fire which were blazing with the flame of fire. First, he started to barb for those heads as everything must first start from them. But I was very surprised to see that all of these heads were shouting with joy as these clippers of fire were touching their heads instead of crying. Again

105

Barbing Day in the Town of Short Ghosts

it was this day I noticed carefully that uncountable beetles, bees, wasps and many other kinds of biting insects were living inside the hair of these heads as their homes and also their mother's head was full up with numerous small birds which built their nests inside the hair of her head as on the trees. Having barbed all the heads and their mother then he started barbing for the short ghosts. But after he barbed half of them all the heads reported to their mother that they were feeling hungry, then she ordered those half who had been already barbed to go and kill an animal from the bush, so at this stage I had a chance and mixed with those who had been already barbed as if I had barbed my own too. So it was this way I saved myself from barbing my head with the clippers of fire.

One day, when I was seriously sick, I was detailed to be at home by the short ghosts to be serving the mother with anything that she wanted to do. I was greatly surprised to say that it was that day I knew that she was selling the flash fire of her eyes to other kinds of ghosts who were coming from the various towns to buy it, and a flash was worth a heavy amount of ghosts' money.

I become an
Aggressor for Ghosts

The very day that I completed three years in this town, the "flash-eyed mother" got a letter and warrant about me from the town that I escaped to her.

But when the mother received the letter she was very annoyed and replied with passion that—"I am ready for war or for any consequence." Then both parties arranged the day that they would meet on their battle-field for seven days to come at that time. But before the day arrived "flash-eyed mother" had sent for all the soldiers of "Wraith-Island" who were uncountable in numbers and also sent for the following wonderful and curious creatures:— "Spirit of prey" who is fighting with the flood of light of his single eyes, "Invisible and invincible Pawn" who fought and won the "Red- creatures" in the "Red-town" for the "Palm-Wine Drinker" when he was living in the "Red-town", and all the fearful and harmful prominent creatures as:— White long creatures, Hungry creature, Shapeless-creatures, and also the "Palm wine tapster", who is living in the Deads' town, who gave the wonderful egg to the Palm-Wine Drinker came too. So all of them had gathered in this town (13th town) before the day came. When the day arrived "flash-eyed

107

mother" gave a wonderful short gun to every one of the
heads of her body, then to the other creatures, after that
to all the short ghosts and me as well, and she took the
biggest gun for herself and also gave a sword to every one
of us in addition.

After this the whole of us were going to the battle-
field, so she was following us as a commander. It was this
day I first saw her stand up and walk away from the
same place that I met her since the three years I came
there, and it was this day I noticed that over four thousand more heads were still hid under her body and all
were exceedingly glad when they were exposed to the
fresh air since the last century when the "Secret Society
of Ghosts" celebrated last. So as the whole of us were
marching hastily to the battle-field that morning because
we had kept late, all these heads were making various
fearful noises with louder voices along the way, even the
rest of us could not hear any other creatures' voices
except their own which nearly made us become deaf.

Before we reached the field the other party had reached
there before us. But immediately we reached there we
started to shoot guns at the enemies and using the swords,
and they were also shooting us. As this fight was so
serious nobody could eat, sleep or rest for three days and
nights. But when we were hiding in a hiding-place at
night or at any time from the enemies all these heads
would not stop making noises until the enemies would
suspect us and then start to shoot us to death. And as it
was a powerful war, so, through the noises of these heads
all the hero-ghosts who were fighting the enemies with
us were killed and also many of the heads were cut away

from their mother's body with swords, except their mother who was fighting on fiercely with her big gun until the "Invisible and Invincible Pawn" who had disappeared for a little while came and killed some of the enemies until the rest escaped to their town. After that he woke up all the hero-ghosts with all the short ghosts who had been killed by the enemies. But to my surprise as all these heads had been cut down to the ground all were still crying to their mother. Of course, the "Invisible and Invincible Pawn" replaced them back on their mother's body, and this means the 13th town won the victory.

After we won the war the whole of us were gladly marching to the town. But as the "Invisible and Invincible Pawn" woke up all the dead soldiers and replaced their heads which were cut off by the enemies to their necks and as my own was cut off as well, so he mistakenly put a ghost's head on my neck instead of mine. But as every ghost is talkative, so this head was always making various noises both day and night and also smelling badly. Whether I was talking or not it would be talking out the words which I did not mean in my mind and was telling out all my secret aims which I was planning in mind whether to escape from there to another town or to start to find the way to my home town as usual. All these secret thoughts were speaking out by this inferior head whenever I stood before "flash-eyed mother" and also telling lies against me every time that I am abusing her because I did not understand the language of the short ghosts. At the same time that I discovered that it was not my own head which was

109

mistakenly put on my neck, so I reported the matter to the mother, but she simply replied—"Every head is a head and there is no head which is not suitable for any creature." So I was carrying the earthly body with the head of a ghost about until the "faithful mother", the inhabitant of the "white-tree", who is faithful to all creatures came and settled the misunderstandings between the two parties when she heard information that there was a war between them, but it was very late before she heard about this war. Having settled the misunderstanding for them I begged her respectfully to replace my own head back on my neck instead of this one which belongs to a ghost. So she agreed and interchanged it for my original head at once, if not I should be still carrying the head of a ghost about throughout my life time. But at the same time she had settled the misunderstanding for both parties (12th town and 13th town) then she went back to her "white-tree" with the "faithful-hand" who accompanied her as a guard and she inspected the "guard of honour" which was specially arranged for her by the "flash-eyed mother" before she went away.

It was this day I knew that this "flash-eyed mother" is the mother of the "Invisible and invincible Pawn" who is the ruler of all the animal creatures and non-living creatures which he could command to become alive in all bushes of the curious creatures, and it was also this day he washed his mother who warmed the water with which to wash her body with the flash fire of her eyes as the water was too cold for her. Having washed his mother he went back to his bush which is near the "Red-town" which had been ruined long ago when the "Palm-

110

I become an Aggressor for Ghosts

Wine Drinker" was living there with the "Red-creatures".

After the war was over all the short ghosts and I continued our usual work as hunters. At this time I was illtreated by all these short ghosts with the "flash-eyed mother" and also all the heads of her body as I was the aggressor of the war which ruined some of them and their opponents as well. So by that my mind was not at rest to live there any longer except to continue to look for the way to my home town which I had left for about eighteen years, as I was remembering my mother at this time always. But as I was at that time near to become a full ghost and did not care for any ghost again, because I had seen many of their secrets except the "Secret Society of Ghosts" which is celebrating or performing every century, so whenever I was following the short ghosts to the bush in which we were killing the animals, I would go farther than them.

The Super Lady

One day, I travelled to every part of this bush if perhaps I might see the way to my town, but instead of seeing the way I saw an antelope. When I was about to shoot him with the gun, he was running away and I myself was chasing him to kill him until he reached a big tree then he ran to the other side of it which debarred me from seeing him, but as I was a little distance from this tree I thought within myself to approach it before I would shoot him. Having approached the tree before I could touch the trigger of my gun there appeared a very beautiful lady and as I was startled immediately I saw that it was that antelope changed to this lady, then I stopped suddenly and looked at her with doubtful and fearful mind that perhaps it was the "flash-eyed mother" changed like this, so that I might not escape from her as I was thinking in my mind. But as I stood and trembled in the place she was waving her right hand as a signal to throw the gun down and I did so at the same moment because of fear. Although if she did not give such sign I would not be able to shoot her at all as an animal. Though it was clear to me that she was an antelope in form at the first time that I saw her when running to that tree. Again I was greatly surprised that it was in my presence

112

she took away the antelope skin from her body and hid it inside a hole which was at the foot of that tree.

Having thrown the gun down then she was waving the hand again to me to come to her at the same place that she stood. Of course, when she was doing so I refused to go, I told her—"No, I cannot come to you, because you are a wonderful and terrible antelope who changed to a lady in my presence."

After that she came to me for herself and asked—"Will you marry me?" but I replied—"Not at all!" Then she held both my hands by force and looking at my face which was nearly touching her own which was as fresh as an angel's face, and she asked again with a lofty smiling face and solemn voice—"Why do you dislike marrying me?" But I replied that I am an earthly person. When she heard so she said—"I prefer to marry an earthly person more than the other creatures." After she said so, she told me to follow her and I followed her at a very low walking speed, because she was fearful to me, but she did not leave my hands because perhaps I might run away from her, and it is truth.

Within a few minutes when I noticed that she was not a harmful ghostess, then I thought within myself to follow her to her town, perhaps if I begged her to show me the way to my town she would agree. But having travelled with her to a distance of about one and an half miles we entered a town, and immediately we entered there I asked her for the name of the town, she replied that it is a nameless town. After a while we reached her house and then entered it, but there was nobody living with her.

113

In the Nameless-town

So immediately we entered the house she swept every part of it and then decorated it. After that she put water in the bath-room, then I went to bathe and before I finished she had put down clothes. Having taken off the animal skin which I wore she took it and hid it in an unknown place and I wore the clothes, but when I looked at myself in a big mirror which was in the parlour I could not identify myself again for the beauty that the clothes added to me and it was this day I believed that clothes are very important for the body, because as I wore it my appearance looked as fresh as an earthly person. Then I asked her where she got the clothes, as all the ghosts are not using earthly clothes, she replied that she got them from the earthly witches who are coming to her father's town for "witch-meetings". Having decorated the house or all the rooms, she went to the kitchen at once and cooked the food which was exactly the same as the earthly food. But I could comb my hair finish before she had put the food on the table in the dining room, then we ate it together. As this food was prepared in the method which earthly people prepare their food, so I ate it to my entire satisfaction, because it was that day I first ate the food which was prepared as good as this since I entered the Bush of Ghosts. Having finished with this food, we went to the parlour and then she brought drinks of all kinds, then both of us started to drink them, and then she started to tell me her story as follows:—

"My mother is a lame ghostess who can only creep about instead of walking. She is born and bred in the 7th town of ghosts and my father is also a native of the 6th town of ghosts which is about two hundred miles distance from this Nameless-town. He is the most powerful wizard among all the wizards in both the Bush of Ghosts and in the earthly towns. And my mother is also the most powerful of all the witches in both the Bush of Ghosts and in the earthly towns. Therefore, for this reason, both are selected by all witches and wizards to be their heads and to be giving orders to every one of them. So by that all of them are coming from every town of ghosts and from every earthly town as well every Saturday to my father's house where there is a special big hall which is built for this meeting. But as both my mother and father are their heads, so we shall prepare all kinds of food and drinks before their arrival at my father's town every Saturday.

"After they eat and drink, they will start to sing the song of witches and wizards, after this they will pray the prayer of the wizards and witches, then the meeting will start, but the most important of their discussions are on those who are not their members as how to rob and wreck them and to lodge the complaints of those who have offended them before my father and mother who will either give them the order to kill their offenders or not. Of course, they will wait and hear the last order from them before going back to their various towns. But if

my father and mother do not order them to do any harm
to those who they bring the complaint of, they must not
do any harm to them, but if both give them the order
to harm or kill them so immediately they return to their
towns they will kill them.

"One day, when I sat down with my father discussing
a matter with him, to my surprise, there I saw an earthly
old woman who is a witch or one of their members come
to my father and started to lodge complaints:— 'One of
my neighbours who is depending on her only son called
me a "witch" which is an insult to us, but for this I will
kill her only son who is taking care of her as a revenge,
so that she will not get anyone to assist her in her need
and she will have nobody to look after her again, and she
shall be in sorrow and hunger throughout her life.'
Having finished the complaint, then she hesitated and
expected which order will be given her by my mother
and father. So my father and mother decided the complaint in their minds within themselves for some minutes
then both ordered the complainant to go and kill the
only son of the woman who offended her and without
hesitation she disappeared. But as this was a great surprise to me immediately she disappeared I told my father
that—'this is a sin' and I reminded him again that—
'you ordered her to go and kill the son on whom his
mother depends?' But he replied—'Yes, I do believe
before you say that it is a sin, even it is more than a sin
or worse, because I am living on such evil works and you
are living on it as well through me and I do not care for
any kind of punishment which God might give me about
it, because I prefer evil works more than godly works and

116

In the Nameless-town

I am sure that I shall go direct to the everlasting fire which is the most hot and the most severe punishment. Even these evil works will appear as well on my "Will" that you are the one who have the right to inherit it after my death.' But when he said that I will inherit all his evil works whenever he dies, I told him at once that— 'I shall not do any evil work throughout my life-time in this Bush of Ghosts.'

"Again, one night, my father and mother entered into a private room which is in a dark corner of the house, then both were discussing within themselves with a low voice whether to kill me next week for their wizard and witch meeting which is very near, because it is our turn to prepare food for our members who will attend the meeting according to our rule, as they have no other daughter or son who is to be killed and cooked and presented to our members, because every one of them will do so whenever it is his or her turn and it is not fair enough to depart away from this rule because of their daughter. So, therefore, as from this night they would not allow me to go anywhere and not to hear about this 'secret arrangement' at all, so that I may not run away from home. But as the time that both of them were discussing this matter within themselves was dark so they did not know that I hid near them and heard all their sayings and also heard the very day that they will kill me. But when the day that they arranged within themselves remained three days, all the wizards and witches were arriving in large number to my father's house from all the towns of ghosts and from all the earthly towns.

"But my grandmother, who is the native of the

In the Nameless-town

'Hopeless-town' which is the 5th town of ghosts and who is at present in the everlasting fire, had given me the power of a 'Superlady' before she was imprisoned in that fire for a little mistake she did to H.M. the King of ghosts. So through this power I had the opportunity to change to an invisible bird early in the morning that my father and mother would kill me, then I packed all my belongings, after that I bade both of them invisibly 'good-bye' and then I came to live permanently in this Nameless-town, which belongs only to women, and since that day I am not appearing to them personally but changing to a kind of a creature, because they would kill me as they are still looking for me to kill, because they have no other son or daughter to kill for their members, as it is a great pain to them if they cannot fulfil the order made for themselves and this rule cannot be cancelled, as uncountable members have killed their sons or daughters when it was their turn.

"Now, my earthly husband, I have the wonderful power to change to any form of creature as I sit with you on the same chair in this parlour." But when she said so, I told her to change to some form at that moment to let me see. Then she said—"look at me carefully." First, she became an antelope with two short horns on its head, secondly a lioness and roared at me several times so that I nearly died for fear, thirdly, a big boa constrictor which made me fear most when she was coiling round my body, especially when it opened the mouth very wide as if it wanted to swallow me, and after this a tigress and jumped on me at the same time, after this she jumped away from my head and was jumping from room to room, having stopped jumping about in the rooms and house, then without hesitation she jumped outside the town, she was chasing fowls about in the town. After some minutes she killed two of the fowls and brought them by mouth to the house, then she came back to me on the same chair that I sat on, after that she changed to a lady as usual, and to my surprise she was on the same chair as before she started to use her supernatural powers and also held the two fowls which she killed outside with her hands.

Then she started another conversation with me for a few minutes before she went to the kitchen with the two fowls, she roasted both, after that she brought them to me with tea and bread. So we ate them together. But before we finished with all these things it was about ten o'clock in the night. Having rested for about an hour and when she noticed that I was feeling sleepy, then she went to the bedroom, she stretched many costly clothes on the bed, after that she called me to enter the room, but when I dangled one of my feet on the door of this room as a step and when I looked how this room was decorated and also how the bed was decorated and then looked at the bed itself how it was made with the finest and most attractive patterns which could be found in this Bush of Ghosts so I insisted on entering the room, but I was simply suggesting in my mind that—"Is this for me? Am I going to sleep on this fine bed on which only a king can sleep?" Because I was afraid to enter this room as it was beautified by all kinds of costly decorations, as all of them could be only made with supernatural power, because an ordinary creature could not make them attractively like that. But after she called me for several times to come inside the room to sleep on the bed, but I stayed at the door looking at both bed and decorations with much surprise, then she came to me and held my hand as smooth as a delicate thing and then drew me very gently and gradually into the room. Then I hesitated again to touch or to sleep on this bed, but when she saw that I did not attempt to sleep on it, so she pushed me on it for herself very gently as a breakable article. As I lay my body on this bed and felt how it was very easy for me, so I sprang up suddenly to go out of the room.

But at the same time that she saw me that I wanted to get down and go out of this room she pressed me on it with all her power for about one hour before my body and mind became at rest, and it was at that night I believed that—"clean places are driving a dirty person away as if it will hurt him." But still I was unable to sleep as I was always thinking in mind how she had been changing herself to various fearful animals and also thinking that perhaps—"She may change again to another form and kill me in the midnight." But having watched her for some hours and believed that she had no such harmful aim in mind at all, then I fell asleep unnoticed. Again to my great surprise there were "all-coloured lights" which lighted and shone as diamonds on to every part of this house, even I tried my best to find out from where the lights were coming, but it was in vain, because it was not quenched both day and night. As it surprised me greatly I asked her about it, she replied —"the power of lights is among my supernatural powers."

In the Nameless-town

This is how I married for the second time in the Bush of Ghosts, but I was not baptized with fire and hot water as I was in the 8th town of ghosts when I married for the first time, and this was easier than that, because we did not go to any church, but she is a "super-lady" who has the power to do everything. So I was unable to tell her some of my stories before I slept that night.

Before she woke me up early in the morning, she had put out the water, and soap which had a sweet and lofty smell; of course, it is in the Bush of Ghosts such soap could be found, even it is only from this "super-lady" it could be found, as it belongs only to her, then the sponge which was as fluffy as cotton, she put them in the bath-room which was as clean as a food plate. After that she woke me up, because if not I would not be able to wake for myself as this bed was so easy for me. Having taken my bath, then I went to the dressing room where she combed my hair for me, she powdered my face and also rubbed my body with a kind of sweet smelling oil. Then from there to the dining-room, so we drank tea together. After we drank the tea, she brought some cold drinks. When I was drinking it she left me there and went away, after a few minutes she returned with two maids who would be helping her to do all the housework. Having given them work to do, then she came to me in the parlour and sat down on the chair which was touching my own which was an easy-chair with cushions. Then she told me with a very cool lofty voice and smiling face to tell her my story which I related very shortly.

After this, one of the maids or servants came and called us for chop which was rice, etc. Having finished with the food, we drank some of the cold drinks which were always in the ice, after this, both of us went all round the town and also to a village which is not more than two miles away from the Nameless-town.

Where Woman Marries Woman

When we went round this Nameless-town before we went to the village, there I noticed carefully that all the inhabitants are ladies and women, no single man is living there or coming there at all and to my surprise all these ladies and women have long brown moustaches which resemble that of he-goats, the moustaches are under their lower jaws, so every woman married a lady, because there are no men to marry them. But when I asked the "Super-lady" or my wife—"Why all the ladies and women have moustaches in this town like he-goats?" she replied—"those women with moustaches had been betrayed by their husbands after their marriage, but now none of them could marry any male again except to marry ladies as husbands." After we took a stroll round the village and saw many terrible and wonderful things for some hours, then we came back home. Having rested and drank some drinks as a refreshment, then we slept till the evening.

When I completed the period of eight months with her I told her that I want to know her father and mother who are wizard and witch and also her grandmother's town who is the native of the Hopeless-town. After a few weeks that I had advised her like this, we left home and there remained only those two maids at home. But we travelled for a week before we saw the town of her father at a distance of five miles, then she told me to stop, so both of us stopped near a tree whose leaves were shaking with powerful speed. Then she told me that she wanted to change herself to a goat and said furthermore that if she appeared personally to her father and mother they would catch her to be killed for their "witch and wizard members", because both of them had promised to kill her for them. After a few minutes she used her super-natural power and changed at once to a goat with a strong rope on its neck, then she told me to hold the rope and pull her along the way. She was directing me whenever I wanted to miss the way and I understood all her sayings as she was changed to the goat, but nobody could hear her voice, except me.

When we reached the town she directed me to her father's house in which we met over three thousand witches and wizards members who were holding an important meeting at that time, then we stood near them and looked at every one of the members. Of course we did not enter the house because she only showed them to me. I saw her father and mother sat on the higher chairs in the centre of these members talking to them. To my surprise I saw many old men and women of my home town who were tight friends to my father and I was greatly surprised to see them in this meeting, be-cause I did not know how they managed to be there, but I did not let them see me. After a while she told me in the same voice to let us go, so we left there for her grandmother's town. Having left that town at a distance of about a mile, then she changed to the lady as before,

124

after that she started to tell me the story of some of the wizard and witch members' witchcrafts and wizardcrafts, that they can travel all round the whole world within a minute and they have power on everything and furthermore all of them have no good thoughts except evil thoughts both day and night, even those who are worshipping the heavenly God are also their enemies. But she did not change to any form again until we entered the town of her grandmother.

Hopeless-town

Having entered this wonderful town which is the
Hopeless-town, we went straight to her grandmother's
house in which we met many ghosts and ghostesses who
received us with gladness because they are her family.
But I did not see her grandmother, because she had been
imprisoned inside the everlasting fire. When we entered
this Hopeless-town, she warned me seriously three times
thus—"You must not speak any word with your mouth
but with a shrug of your shoulders. Whenever you are
talking to any ghost in this town you must not raise up
or down your eyelids and also your mouth must not open
at all. If you mistakenly or wilfully break any of these
warnings it would result in a severe punishment for you."
Having warned me like this, I told her that—"I do not
think that I will return without any punishment, because
I shall forget to comply with the whole warnings."
Having warned me like this, she herself stopped talking
with her mouth and I too.

As a matter of fact I noticed well that nobody is talking
by mouth in this town, even if a baby is born on the
same day, he or she would not talk by mouth and also
all their domestic animals as sheep, goats, fowls or all
creatures that are living there are not talking with their
mouths but with the shrug of their shoulders.

Hopeless-town

One day, when my wife with her sister went to visit their grandmother in the everlasting fire in which she was imprisoned over two hundred years, as I remained alone at home I thought within myself to go as far as the centre of this town as a stroll. Having travelled to the centre of the town I stopped and I was gloating at a curious creature whose body was full of large eyes, but as a ghost was passing closely to me, he mistakenly smashed my foot unexpectedly with his heavy foot which had long nails of about half a foot. But as he smashed me, I cried out louder suddenly—"Oh", and those who stood by heard my voice which was very strange to them, because there is no noise of any creature, every part of the town is always calm as if there is nobody living there at all. So as I cried out which is against their law, those who stood by came and held me as a thief, then they took me to their king who sat on a fearful idol which was moulded with yellow and red clay or mud, because it is on such a seat that the king of this town must be sitting whenever he wants to judge a very serious case. Then he was asking me these questions with a shrug of his shoulders as follows:— "Who are you?" But as I did not understand what he was asking me with the shrug of the shoulders, so to set myself free from the punishment I began to reply as well with my own shrug of the shoulders as he was doing, which means to him—"you are a bastard king." And again, on the same spot that I stood before him I mistakenly raised up and down the lids of my eyes which means—"you are fool," and this is contrary to the law of this town. Again I mistakenly opened down my mouth at the same moment, and this means to

127

them—"I shun you away." But when all the ghosts and ghostesses who stood by saw this again, all were shouting with the shrug of their shoulders in such a way that the shoulders were nearly cut off, this means—"Ah! you are abusing the king."

So as these three rules are very important offences for them in this town, and also all the three are not pardonable as my wife had already told me before we entered the town, so the king ordered those who brought me to him to take me to the purgatory which is near the town to throw me inside it as a punishment. But as these ghosts were dragging me mercilessly along the road to the purgatory instead of letting me walk with my feet, so, luckily, at that time, my wife with her sister were returning from the place that they had gone to visit their grandmother and it was on this road they were travelling along to the town. Immediately both of them met these ghosts dragging me along, they knew already that I had made mistakes, so both started to beg these ghosts not to put me inside the purgatory, and bribed them with some amount before I was released. But at the same time that I was released, my wife and myself did not return to that town again, except her sister. So we started from there to return to our Nameless-town, but it was a queer road we took instead of the one on which we travelled to that town. If my wife and her sister had not met these ghosts on the way as they were dragging me to the purgatory, I should have perished before she would know. This is how we left the Hopeless-town.

On the Queer Way to Homeward

On our queer way to homeward we visited many towns and villages. But this queer way is farther than the way on which we travelled when going to the town of my wife's father and her grandmother's town and also we spent more time before we reached our Namelesstown than when going. We visited the towns and villages as follows:— We first visited a village which is near the 26th country of ghosts. All the inhabitants of this village were not more than forty thousand ghosts and ghostesses. All of them were in peace and in pleasure always. They were harmless to either earthly persons or to other kinds of creatures. We reached there at about ten o'clock in the night and yet they received us with gladness. Before an hour that we reached there they had cooked food and brought it to us with drinks, after that, all of them sat round us outside, then merriment began in which jokes, dance, clapping and the drums of ghosts were included.

None of them sleep till the morning but amused us throughout, especially the "jocose-ghostess" who was among them, she was joking in such a way that if a sick man is hearing her jokes he would be healed at once without using any medicine. As all of them were wealthy in corn, sheep, fowls and foxes, so they gave us one fowl, a fox, some quantity of corn and a lamb which was not more than five months old as gifts, because my wife informed them that I am her husband and all of them were pleased to be so. After these gifts then we went round to their houses and thanked them greatly for their kindness.

Then we left there at about nine o'clock in the morning and all of them led us to a short distance as if we are a king before they returned to their village. But having travelled to a distance of seven miles away from that village we reached a wide river which crossed our way.

Lost or Gain Valley

Having crossed the river we travelled to a distance of four miles from that river till we reached a deep valley which is crossed this queer way. A very slender stick was put across it with which to be crossed by everyone, but there was no other single stick near that area. But when we reached this "Lost or Gain Valley" we saw a notice-board on which all these warnings are written in the ghosts' language as follows:—"Put all the clothes on your body with loads down here before climbing this valley." And I did not understand it. But as this slender stick was so slender, so we tried all our best to climb it with clothes on our bodies and failed before we understood what is written on the board, then my wife took all the clothes off her body and put them down, then she first crossed it. This means the slender stick was not strong enough for a person to climb it with clothes on their body. After my wife crossed it easily without clothes on her body, then I did as she did and I crossed it easily as well. All of our dress cost more than £100. Not knowing that the meaning of the name of this valley which is— "Lost or Gain Valley" means as we put all our clothes down at this first edge before crossing it, it is so for those who are travelling towards us from the opposite direction who should put down all the clothes off their bodies at

131

the second edge as well before they could climb it and after climbing it then they will take any clothes that they meet there and wear them instead of their own which they leave before climbed it. Perhaps the clothes that they might meet there might cost more than their own, so it is their gain and if the one that they meet there are not worth their own it is also their loss.

So having made ourselves naked and climbed to the second edge, then we stopped there and waited, perhaps a cloth-seller might come to pass at that time, so that we might buy some clothes from him or her to wear at that spot and then to continue our journey, because we did not meet any clothes at this second edge and we could not travel along the road without clothes on our bodies. But after some hours that we had been waiting there for a cloth-seller, a couplet ghosts, wife and husband, came. They wanted to climb this valley to the other edge. But as both are the natives of that area so they knew how they are climbing it every time and without hesitation they took away all the animal skins that they wore from their bodies and put them down there, then both of them climbed the valley to the second edge. Having reached there they did not waste time, but the husband wore my costly clothes as trousers, shirt, tie, socks, shoes, hat, golden ring with my costly wrist-watch. After this his wife wore my wife's clothes as—underwear, gown, golden beads, rings, hat, shoes, wrist-watch, after that she handled her (my wife's) lofty hand-bag, and then both of them went away without hesitation. But when they did so and went away then we quite understood what we should do. So we wore their own as well. But it is a great pity and loss that their own were only the animal skins which were worth nothing and the worst part of it, it was just a baby's clothes on our bodies, because it was not the size for us at all and also made us more ugly and fearful to any creature to meet us on the way. So it was our loss and it was their gain. And it was after we left that area we heard that no stranger would cross this valley without loss, because all the ghosts and ghostesses of that area are very poor and only living on this kind of exchange.

Then we kept going as usual with our shameful appearance which did not make us feel happy as before. But I am not satisfied as somebody told us that those ghost etc. of that area could not lose but gain. So I am still eager to find out the right way of how to cross this "Lost or Gain Valley" without any loss except gain. "Do you know?" After we had travelled again on this "queer-way" to about two miles in that valley, then we entered into a town at about eight o'clock in the night, because we had wasted much time at the valley, but as we were totally tired, so we went to a ghost's house who is well-known to my wife, and we slept there till the morning. But as we wanted to spend a few days there to rest, so we cooked our food early in the morning, then we ate it to our satisfaction.

Having left there we did not branch again to any town but straight to our Nameless-town. Immediately we reached home we ate the food which had been prepared for us by the two maids who deputed for us at home. After that we left the dining-room for the parlour and then started to drink and also tell my wife some of the earthly news which she is always interested to hear every time.

Son Divides Us

When I completed the period of a year with her, then she conceived and some months later she delivered a male baby who resembled me with half of his body and the rest his body resembled his mother. The naming ceremony of this baby was performed after the third day he was born according to the ghosts' custom. All the prominent ghosts with ghostesses came in large numbers for this grand ceremony. They gave him the ghosts' name which I could not write or pronounce, of course, I myself gave him an earthly name which is—"OKOLE-BAMIDELE", the meaning is—"you cannot follow me to my home." I gave him this name according to his nature which is half ghostess and half earthly person.

Within six months that he was born he had grown up to the height of four feet and some inches. He could do everything in the house. But the worst part of it is that whenever I talked to him to do something, he would do it in the half method that ghosts are doing all their things and then in the half method that the earthly persons are doing everything. So I hated him for this habit, because I wanted him to do everything completely in the method that the earthly persons are doing everything and also his mother hated him for the half method that he was doing everything, because she wanted him to do everything in the full way that ghosts are doing their own things. She wanted him to be acting as a full ghost as herself and I myself wanted him to be acting as a full earthly person as I am. So by this reason the love which was between ourselves was vanishing away gradually until when I completed the period of four years with her.

One night I was joking with her that—"earthly people are superior to the ghosts and ghostesses or all other creatures." But when she heard this from me she was extremely annoyed. Without asking me the reason about what I said, she simply went to an unknown place that she kept the animal skin which was on my body when she met me. But as she had taken it from me and hid it in an unknown place at the time I followed her from the bush to her house on the day she met me in the bush, so she brought it and took away all the clothes that she gave me from my body and then gave me my animal skin to wear. But when I saw her rude attitude I was greatly annoyed as well, then I took it from her and wore it as before I met her. After that she drove me away from that town. Which means I come back to my former condition. So I left there at two o'clock in the midnight to an unknown place, because I did not know any part of that area or to hear any news about any town which is near there to go direct and shelter myself throughout that night from any dangerous ghost or creature.

Having left her and travelled in the bush to a short distance then I remembered to continue to be looking for the way to my home town as I had forgotten that for a while, because of love. So this is how I left the "Superlady" who was my wife because of our son. After the fifth month that I had left her and roamed about in the bush both day and night, and nobody could identify me again that I am not a ghost, because I was then nearly become a full ghost and was doing everything that ghosts are doing and also speaking the language of ghosts fluently as if I was born in the Bush of Ghosts, so through this language that I could speak and understand I was always protected from uncountable merciless ghosts as it was hard for some of them to believe that I am an earthly person.

One night, at about eleven o'clock there I entered a town unnoticed. All the inhabitants of this town had slept very early, because it was in the rainy season, again it was raining from morning of that day till the evening, as this is always happening in the Bush of Ghosts. But when I went as far as to the centre of this town perhaps I might discover the fire in which to roast a very small yam which a ghost gave me after he slapped my ear warmly ten times before giving it to me, because yams were very scarce to get in some parts of the Bush of Ghosts. Having given me this yam he mounted me and rode me about for three days and nights before he released me.

So as I was roaming up and down in this town to get the fire I was easily arrested as a burglar. Because many of their houses had been burgled a week previously before I entered there, so the guard-ghosts who arrested me thought that I was one of the burglars or coming to burgle another house again and furthermore, when they saw the small yam which I wanted to roast in the fire

136

some of them held me tightly for the rest who were beating me repeatedly with clubs in respect of this yam alone. After that they took me to their guard-room to keep me safely till the morning before they would put the case in the court. I was very surprised to see that I was totally covered by mosquitoes in this guard-room so that nobody could see many parts of my body and it was in this town I saw that mosquitoes are worshipped, kept or tamed and regarded as their god, they are respecting them as their doctors and none of them could live in any town where there are no mosquitoes as they are recognising them purifying their blood to the good state. There I noticed as well that they have several special shrines in which they are worshipping them and scheduled the term of festival two times in a year. But if they discover in any year that mosquitoes are less than previous years it would be bad luck for them and at once they would make a special sacrifice in these shrines to increase mosquitoes in abundance so that they would fill everywhere in the town.

So it was not yet eight o'clock in the morning before I was taken to the court which was specially arranged for my case and the judge did not ask me any question before he judged it and then sentenced me to sixteen years' imprisonment with hard labour. Then I was taken to their prison yard in which all kinds of severe punishments are always awaiting offenders. Immediately I was taken there and handed to one of the chief warders who are in charge of the yard, then two junior warders were preparing fire inside a big oven in which I would spend the sentence passed on me. I would be entering inside this oven from five o'clock every morning and coming out at seven o'clock every evening till the term would be expired. But as it was hard labour, so instead of resting for some time till I would enter it again at five o'clock in the morning I would be collecting charcoal into this oven again with which to make another fire. So by that I would have no rest for a minute until the term would be expired. I was very surprised that all ghosts are thinking that earthly persons could not die as they themselves could not die. Because to imprison themselves and other creatures in the fire are very common in the Bush of Ghosts.

Immediately these two warders had prepared the fire and told me to be getting ready to enter inside it and when I was preparing to enter it, luckily, it was that day their king should come to visit the yard and he entered it at that time without noticing all the warders, so he saw me stand closely before the oven or fire with my eyes which were as wild as a wild animal's eyes when chasing his prey with hunger and much difficulty. So he approached me at the same moment he saw me and asked whether I knew him. But I replied—"I did not." Then he said— "I am your son and your wife who is 'Superlady' is my mother." Then I knew him very well after he had explained himself to me. After that, he ordered some of the warders to lead me to his palace and they did so. So I was very glad that this king is my son and also saved me entering the fire. Having inspected the prison yard all round, then he came back to the palace, he told his attendants to give me food with all kinds of drinks.

Having spent some years with him, then I told him to

tell me the right way to my home town. But as none of the ghosts is too young to persuade he told me—"Yes, I know the right way to your town, but to tell you such a thing is against our rule in this Bush of Ghosts." When he said so, I explained that if he tells me the way and if I go, I will be spending only a few days in my town before I will be coming back to visit him regularly, but yet he insisted on the first point that he raised. When it was a week later after he refused to tell me the way, then I told him that I want to continue to find out the way. Of course, when heard so, he begged me not to leave him, but I myself refused totally to stay with him as he refused to tell me the way. So I left him and started to find the way.

After the eighth month that I had left him there I reached the 4th town of ghosts at about twelve o'clock midnight. But I did not enter it at that time so that the guard ghosts might not catch me there as a thief as in the town in which my son is the king. When it was eight o'clock in the morning then I entered the town and went direct to the king, I reported that I am a foreigner in his town, because at that time I could explain myself fully before any ghost as I said that before I left my wife or the "Superlady" she taught me the language of the ghosts. So by that I explained before this king that:— it is disgraceful to hear that the earthly people are always abusing all the ghosts and now I volunteer myself to go to their towns to warn them of this abuse and I shall be glad if he will tell me the right way to any of the nearest earthly towns. After I explained to him like this, he waited for half an hour, of course, he could not identify me that I am not a ghost and he did not understand my trick that I am only to find out the right way from him. Before he started to reply my request he told a ghost to give me food with drinks as he noticed that I was feeling hunger at that time. As I was eating the food, then he was telling me—"I will tell you the right way to the earth to go and warn them if you can volunteer your left arm to me. Because one arm of the most beautiful of all my wives had been cut away before I married her, so that I will fit your own there, because it is our rule in this town that any king who is on the throne must not marry any armless or amputy as wife. And one of the rest of the wives had told this secret to all the chiefs, kingmakers and the prominent ghosts of this town that I married an armless ghostess as wife. The reason why she leaked out the secret is only because I love this armless wife more than the rest of them. All the chiefs, and kingmakers, with the prominent ghosts had come and asked me about the matter in secret whether it is true, but I told them that it is not true, because if I tell them frankly that it is true they will kill me. But when I told them that it is not the truth, then they told me that in five days to come they will come to the palace, then all my wives will come out and sit in a row, after that every one of them will be grinding corn on the stone with two hands in the presence of the chiefs, kingmakers and the prominent ghosts, but if any one of the wives cannot produce two hands or arms to grind the corn, then they will kill me on the same spot, as I am against the rule and now it remains only two days to come for the test." But as he said that if I could volunteer one of my arms to fit on his wife's arm which was cut off, then he would tell me the right way to the earthly towns, so I was very glad to hear that.

Then I told him to call the armless wife to show me the arm which had been cut off, when she came and showed me the arm, so I measured it with a kind of ghosts' rope in such a way that the measurement was equal with the one which was not cut. After this, I went to a bush which is near that palace with this rope, and moulded another arm with mud which was the same size with the rope, then I brought it and told this armless wife to stretch the other half which remained with her, so I let the artificial arm touch the part that remained with her, after that I performed a kind of juju which was given to me by a "triplet ghost". Immediately I performed the juju the artificial arm joined together with the rest and at the same time it became exactly the natural arm, even nobody could believe that it was cut off before, and none of the wives who hated her knew that she had got complete arms until the day of the inspection was reached and all of them were still proud that they have complete arms and were also telling this armless wife in the proverbial way that she is near to be killed with the king who loved her only.

When the day of this inspection was reached, all the chiefs, kingmakers, with all the prominent ghosts of this town came to the palace, all of them sat in the same row, then they put a flat grinding stone with corn on the front, after that they called all the king's wives out and told them to sit down in a row at a little distance from them and also told the king to sit in the middle. After that they asked the king again—"Is it true that you

141

married an armless ghostess as a wife?" But he replied as usual that he did not marry an armless ghostess as wife at all. Having spoken one of the inspectors started to command every one of these wives to be grinding that corn on the stone with two hands so that the wife who has an arm might be detected. But after all the rest who had complete hands ground the corn with their complete hands successfully, they told the one who was suspected to be armless that it is her turn to grind the corn. But as she was all the while hiding the hand under her cloth till the time she was called, so she got up and approached the stone, but the other wives were still thinking that she would not be able to grind it. So she knelt down and ground the corn successfully with two hands as the other wives. When the rest of the wives with the chiefs, kingmakers and prominent ghosts who were inspectors saw her with two complete hands all were greatly surprised. Then these chiefs, kingmakers and prominent ghosts or inspectors asked the rest of the wives—"Why did all of you tell a lie against the king that he married an armless ghostess as wife?" But when none of them could answer this question, and only looked as dummies, then the inspectors killed all of them, except the one who was supposed to be armless, because it is their rule as well in this town not to tell lies against the king. After all have been killed, then the inspectors went back to their houses. So the beauty of a woman or a lady among ugly women or many ugly ladies is always resulting in extreme hatred, and the hatred sometimes brings good luck to one who is abhorred or hated. Because it was only this beautiful ghostess was then the ruler of the palace with the king after the rest of the wives who hated her greatly for her beauty had been killed.

After a week that I had done this wonderful work to this king and also saved his wife, then I asked him to tell me the right way to the earthly towns as he promised before. But instead of telling me the way he said—"I like you to stay here with me for the period of fifteen years, perhaps the arm may be cut unexpectedly, so that you may rejoin it again." Of course, I did not blame him as he told me to wait for fifteen years, because he did not know that I am not a ghost. Although I believed that my trick would not succeed, then I left there at night without his knowledge and continued my journey as usual, until I entered a very clean town which resembled an earthly town, even at first I thought that it is my town.

I meet my Dead Cousin in the 10th Town of Ghosts

Having entered this 10th town of ghosts all the inhabitants of this town rushed out from their houses to see what happens. Immediately I saw them then I ran directly to one of them who resembled an earthly person among them, but when I approached him he was my dead cousin who had died in my town since I was six and an half years old. Immediately I saw him clearly that he is my dead cousin I ran to his back and held him. After that he told all the inhabitants of this town who came to the scene that I am his junior brother. But when they heard so from him all of them shouted with gladness at a time. After this, I followed him to his house with some of the ghosts to greet him at home. Because all of the inhabitants of this town were respecting him as he is the one who brought Christianity to their town. Having reached home, he told one of his servants to give me food and drinks at once, again many of the prominent ghosts of this town were sending a variety of food and drinks through him to me for "well come". Furthermore, when it was about eight o'clock in the night all the chiefs and king, with famous and prominent ghosts of this town gathered together at the front house

144

of my cousin, then the whole of us started to drink all kinds of ghosts' drinks, we were also dancing, drumming and singing the song of ghosts until daybreak, and this was the "Well come Function". It was that day I saw that some of these ghosts were dancing in such a way until they cut into halves and again both these halves were also dancing until they joined together as usual.

After this "Well come Merriment" ended and when the day broke all of them went back to their houses, but still my cousin was receiving uncountable letters of congratulation, with presents from various towns and villages which were under this 10th town of ghosts, who were unable to come personally. Having gone back to their houses, I told my cousin that I want to sleep as all of us did not sleep throughout that night, so he opened a reserved room, then I slept on a bed which was specially decorated with expensive clothes. Of course, it is only in the Bush of Ghosts such a bed could be found. I woke up at two o'clock p.m., because I had not slept on such a bed since I left my wife the "Superlady" in the Nameless-town. After that I took my bath, then I ate and drank to my satifaction, because in the Bush of Ghosts whenever you eat drinks must follow. Then my cousin started his story after he died before he came and was established in this 10th town as follows:—

"Immediately I died in our town I went to several towns which perhaps would be suitable to establish the Christianity works, but I could not get such a suitable town until I reached here which is suitable. As you know that before I died I was one of the staunch members of the Methodist Church in our earthly town and I am still praying to God that I shall carry on the services until the last day, which is the 'judgement-day' because I could not die again for the second time until that day. At the same time that I came to live in this town, first of all, I went direct to H.M. the King of the Bush of Ghosts and informed him that I want to establish the Christianity works in this 10th town, so he agreed after several meetings to consider this request with himself and his councillors. After this request was approved, the second thing I did, I went round this town, then I found a suitable ground on which I built the first church and it was 90 × 70 ft., the roof was covered with flat bark of the big trees, because there were no iron sheets or other things to use at that time, and then was written on the upper entrance of the main door as follows— 'THE METHODIST CHURCH OF THE BUSH OF GHOSTS.' It was written in bold letters with the white juice of a tree, because there was no paint at that time and also the wall which is mud was painted inside and out with a kind of leaves which yielded the grey colour when ground and mixed with water. Of course, as I was all the while sub-letting a house with a ghost during the time that I was in activity in building the church, so also after it was been completed, although some ghosts helped me. Then I found another suitable ground again and built this house in which we are at present, but it was three months before it was completed with the help of some young ghosts of this town. After that I went round the town on a Saturday evening with a flat hard wood as a bell and told them what is to be doing in that house.

"On Sunday, which was the 1st Sunday to attend or to

hold the 1st service there, I noticed that only two young ghosts attended with me out of about four million ghosts and ghostesses who are living here. Because all of them did not know anything about God or believe that there is God who created them or believe that no other creature is above them. Though, I preached and encouraged those two who attended with me, after that the service closed at 11 a.m. But I did not attempt to hold the evening service on that Sunday. It was a short dead stump of a big tree which has a large hole inside which was beaten as the toll-bell or church-bell whenever it is time for service, because this dead stump is near the church. On Monday, I formed a campaign, I was preaching from house to house, encouraging and explaining what is God to these ghosts until the second Saturday. On Sunday which was the second Sunday, the attendance showed fifty old, thirty-eight young and forty-five child ghosts respectively who attended and all totalled = 133. So, I was exceedingly glad on that day. After the service closed at 11 a.m. I told them that all the young with children should come for Sunday-school at 2 o'clock or if any of the old who like may come as well. Again, the attendance for the Sunday-school showed fifty-seven. Of course the attendance in the evening service was very poor and was only forty-eight in all, because all ghosts like to go to the farms for their food every evening.

"After the sixth month that the church was opened, I converted it to both church and school. I was teaching ghost children of this town how to read and write and also scripture which is the main subject. But there was no paper, chalk or slates on which to write as in the earthly towns so, instead of that I cut a 4 ft. sq. flat bark of a tree as blackboard and also cut 1 ft. sq. for each of the scholars as slates and all were using coal as chalks. As we were using the church in the ordinary day and also on Sunday as a church, then I built a big separate house as church with the help of both scholars and members of the church, because the scholars are making the former one too rough before Sunday. This second building nearly touched the former one. After some years I have had more than fifty ghost teachers out of these scholars and over nine hundred scholars were attending the school regularly. Having trained many bright scholars as teachers and headmasters, then I built over a thousand churches with schools in all provinces which are under this 10th town. So I am using the 10th town as head-quarters for the rest and also the Synod is held here yearly, because I am the bishop at present. My work after the church services is only to be supervising churches and schools. Although there are many supervisors, directors of education and education officers who are carrying on their tasks according to the rules and regula-tions given them to my satisfaction. In my leisure hours, I taught many scholars who had been passed out from the schools sanitary work, surveying, building, first aid nursery work, but only this 'first aid' nursery work I could teach them, because I am not a qualified doctor.

"After all these students had qualified for these various trades and carrying them on successfully to my entire satisfaction, then I introduced new plans of houses and luckily all the ghosts who are the rulers of this town agreed to follow it. Then new houses were built which made this town to link up as the most beautiful town in the Bush of Ghosts. Though it was only disqualified at that time for the hospital which was not established in the town, although there was provision for it but no qualified doctor who could carry on the works."

The second day my cousin took me round the town and I saw many churches, schools, hospitals and many houses which are built in modern styles. But when I asked him about the hospitals who is acting as a doctor and as nurses or who are treating the patients there as he himself is not a doctor, so he replied—"Do you see my wife?" I said—"Yes." Then he told me in short about her as follows—"She is the native of a town in Zulu country, the town which has now been converted to a big city after she had died there. Before she died, she was a well-educated girl and after she had finished her schooling, her father sent her to a part of England as a doctor student, but after she had qualified as a doctor, she returned to her father's town and in the same week that she arrived home she met with an accident and died suddenly as a result of injuries. Having died she left that town, she was going here and there as a dead young person could not stay in a town which belongs to earthly persons, because that is forbidden for all deads and she was roaming about until she reached this town, then we got married as both of us are deads. But as this town is well improved but only disqualified by the hospitals which were not then in it, so as she is a qualified doctor before she died, she established hospitals in this town and acted as the Director of Medical Services. Having trained several thousands of nurses and medical officers."

My Dead Cousin in the 10th Town of Ghosts

Again I asked him these questions:— (1) Who ordained you before you came up to the rank of a bishop? (2) Who is supplying you all kinds of medicines and apparatus which you are using in the hospitals? (3) Who are supplying you all the educational books, religious books as bibles, songs books and papers or stationery, as the flat bark of the trees are no more in use by the scholars? (4) From whom are you getting the iron sheets and all the building materials, as all the houses are no more thatched with grasses and flat bark of the trees? Then he replied as follows—"(1)   As I am carrying on this Christianity work for many years and faithfully to all creatures and did not doubt once for everything that I am doing, so one night, I dreamed a dream and heard the holy voice from heaven that I am ordained as a bishop from heaven as from this night. When the day broke which was Sunday and I explained this news to all the members they confirmed it since that day. (2) Thank you, we are getting the medicines with apparatus for the hospitals from the dead medicine-makers and hospital apparatus-makers who are expert in such works before dying and living in the Deads' town which belongs only to deads. (3) All deads who are the publishers of religious books, educational books and stationery before they died and went to live in the Deads' town are supplying us from there. (4) Deads are supplying us everything that we need here after we had entered into the agreement with them and they are acting for us as the 'Crown Agent' .

Having answered all the four questions, then we came back to the house. After that he called his four daughters

and two sons, after a while his wife who is the Director
of Medical Services came back from the hospitals and
showed me to them and explained how I am related to
him. Those two sons were still attending the school, but
the four daughters had passed out from the school and
also qualified as nurses and doctors.

After the third day that he had told me his stories,
then he told me to give him the home news which went
thus—"After you had died and before I myself entered
into the Bush of Ghosts none of our family die, but one
of them was sick seriously for three weeks before he
became well. After the sixth month that you died a war
of slavery broke into the town and drove me into this
Bush of Ghosts, even I was seven years old before I
entered it. At present I could not definitely say anything
about their condition at home, because I left there over
twenty years ago. So since I left the town my mind does
not rest at all at a time except to return and I am still
looking for the way until I reached here and instead of
seeing the way I was only punished in the bush by the
merciless ghosts. So I am exceedingly glad as I meet you
in this town and I shall be very glad as well if you will
allow me to live with you here for a short period to rest
for some time for all the punishment which I had met
past and then to continue to find the way as before I
reached here or I shall be glad too if you will tell me the
right way direct to the town."

After I told him some of my stories in this Bush of
Ghosts, then he asked this question—"Have you died
before entered this bush?" I replied—"Not at all sir."
But at the same moment that this reply came out of my

mouth, he shouted with his loudest voice "Ah!" together with some ghosts who sat with us at that time. Then he said—"You will not be able to live with deads, of course, as you soon become a full ghost and also hear the language of ghosts, so by that I will teach you until you will qualify to be a full dead person."

After some weeks he handed me to one of the principals of his schools as a new scholar, then I started to learn how to read and write. In the evening my cousin would be teaching me how to be acting as a dead man and within six months I had qualified as a full dead man. And again as I had a quick brain at that time, so I finished my schooling after a few years. Then I was sent without hesitation direct to the Deads' town as a student to learn how to judge cases, as police and also all the branches of the court works. Having become expert in this field, then I returned and started the works. But at the first time we built police stations, courts and prison yards in every part of the town, because these works were not yet established before I reached there. After that I taught many ghosts who had just passed out from the schools all these works and later on I was chosen as the chief judge of the highest court which is the "Assize court". So I was judging all of the important cases which were sent to me from the lower courts.

One day my cousin called me to discuss about his four daughters with the two sons. He asked me who would marry the four daughters, because they are at the ripe age to be married, but no earthly man in any part of the Bush of Ghosts could marry them and again no earthly ladies for the two sons to marry. When he asked me like

152

My Dead Cousin in the 10th Town of Ghosts

this, I told him to let us advertise them on the earthly newspapers several times, perhaps we would get those who would marry them, he agreed to my suggestion and told me to advertise them on the earthly newspapers. "So do you like to marry one of them? If it is so, please, choose any and only one of these numbers—733, 744, 755, 766 and 777, 788 respectively, so that his or her picture may be sent to you or to come to you personally."

Invisible Magnetic Missive
sent to Me from Home

Having been educated and become the chief judge my mind was then at rest, I did not feel to go to my town again, even I determined that I should not go for ever. But one night, when I slept I dreamed a dream which was just as if I was in my home town and also eating with my mother and brother as we were doing before we left each other and I was also playing with my friends as before entered the Bush of Ghosts. So when I woke up in the morning I remembered all these dreams, then I began to feel to go, but however I was putting my mind away from it. When I slept the following night I dreamed the same dream again, but when I woke up in the morning I felt to go my town more than the first time. And the third time that I dreamed again I was unable to eat, play, or feel happy at all, except to go. Even if I walk to any corner it would seem as if I was with my people, doing everything we were doing before I left them. So at this stage I thought of nothing more than to go, because I could not sleep both day and night any more, and I was always dreaming without sleeping or without closing my eyes. Not knowing that my people at home had gone to an earthly fortune teller and asked him whether I am still alive or dead already, but he told them that I am still alive in a bush, but my aim is not to come back to home any more. He said furthermore that I am living with somebody who is taking great care of me. Although he was unable to tell them the real bush that I was in and he could not tell them the kind of the person that I was living with. As he told them that I am still alive, my people simply told him to call me home with the power of his "Invisible Missive Magnetic Juju" which could bring a lost person back to home from an unknown place, how far it may be, with or without the will of the lost person. So having paid him his workmanship in advance, then he started to send the juju to me at night which was changing my mind or thought every time to go home.

Bad-bye Function

But as I could no longer bear to stay with my cousin
except to go, then I told him, but he refused totally at
the first time. When I was pressing him every time and
telling a lie that I want to go and visit a friend of mine
in the 7th town of ghosts, then he allowed me to go,
because I was lean as if I should die within a few days.
So as I was very popular with all ghosts of this 10th town
and environment, when it remained one day for me to
leave there I called all the ghosts of this town to my
cousin's front house for a special function for this "Bad-
bye". But none of them knows that I would not come back
again as it was a "secret function" to all of them. This
function was so greatly performed so that nobody could
sleep till the morning except drinking, dancing various
dances, beating drums and singing. But my cousin was
so sad that he did not appear.

Immediately the day broke I left them there and
started to find the way to my home town as before I met
my cousin in this 10th town of ghosts. This is how I left
them. But as I did not know the right way straight to
my town so this "Magnetic juju" was taking me to every
place in either dangerous bush or not, so I started another
punishment by ghosts. After the ninth month that I
left my dead cousin I reached the 18th town which is

about six hundred miles away from the 10th town. Having reached there a ghost whose throat was always sounding with various voices as a motor horn received me to his house with gladness. His house was on a high rock which is above every house in this town, he was the one who was blowing the horn through his throat to all the ghosts of this town in every hour as a clock and this horn was also waking everyone at five o'clock in the morning. After a week that I arrived to his house I noticed that he was too poor to feed me, because he was very old, even he could not feed himself and had nobody to support him. But as I had already become a real ghost before I left the 10th town, so by that a ghost friend of mine taught me the art of magic, because he did not know that I am an earthly person at that time, otherwise he would not teach me to become a magician. So as I was taught this art before I reached this town, one day, when I thought within myself that this old ghost could not feed me unless I would feed him, therefore I went to a village which is near this 18th town, luckily, I met a ghost magician who was displaying his magical power for the head chief of that village at that time. Then I joined him to display my own as well before these chiefs, as a competition. But when I changed the day to the night, so every place became dark at once, then I told him to change it back to the day as usual, but he was unable. After this I changed him to a dog and he started to bark at everybody, then as my power was above his own the chief with all the scene-lookers gave me all the gifts which were to be shared for both of us. After that I changed him from the dog to a ghost as usual. Then I packed all these gifts and kept going to the 18th town where I came to that village, I did not give him any of the gifts.

Having left this village to a distance of a mile this ghost magician came to me on the way, he asked me to let both of us share the gifts, but when I refused he changed to a poisonous snake, he wanted to bite me to death, so I myself used my magical power and changed to a long stick at the same moment and started to beat him repeatedly. When he felt much pain and near to die, then he changed from the snake to a great fire and burnt this stick to ashes, after that he started to burn me too. Without hesitation I myself changed to rain, so I quenched him at once. Again he controlled the place that I stood to become a deep well in which I found myself unexpectedly and without any ado he controlled this rain to be raining into the well while I was inside. Within a second the well was full with water. But when he wanted to close the door of the well so that I might not be able to come out again or to die inside it, I myself changed to a big fish to swim out. But at the same moment he saw the fish he himself changed to a crocodile, he jumped into the well and came to swallow me, but before he could swallow me I changed to a bird and also changed the gifts to a single palm fruit, I held it with my beak and then flew out of the well straight to the 18th town. Without any ado he changed himself again to a big hawk chasing me about in the sky to kill as his prey. But when I believed that no doubt he would kill me very soon, then I changed again to the air and blew within a second to a distance which a person could not travel on foot for thirty years. But when I changed to my former form at the end of this distance, to my surprise, there I met him already, he had reached there before me and was waiting for me for a long time. Now we appeared personally to ourselves. Then he asked me to bring the gifts, but after both of us struggled for many hours, then I shared the gifts into two parts, I gave him a part, but he insisted to take the whole. However, I gave him all.

Immediately he left me, then I changed to the air again, after I blew far away after him, I stopped on the way on which he would travel to his town, then I changed to a person. Before he could travel to that place I used my magical power. I killed a bush animal, I dug a hole close to this road, after that I cut the head off this animal, I put it upright inside the hole, it faced the road as if it peeped out of the ground alive, having done this, I hid myself near there. After a while he travelled to that place but when he saw this head as it appeared from the ground, he stopped suddenly and looked at it carefully for a few minutes, because it was very curious to him. Then he started to ask this head with fearful mind— "Ah! my lord, here you are?" After that he bowed down respectfully for it for three times, having done so, he was asking it—"Do you want one of these gifts?" But as it did not show any sign of motion, so he threw one of them before it. But as he wanted this head to talk to him, he said again—"Or this is the one you want?" he held the gift, showing it to this head as he was saying so. And threw that as well before it, and it was like this he was doing until he threw all these gifts before it. After that, he laughed louder and ran hastily to his town, he told all the inhabitants with the king that he saw where the "ground has head and eyes" today. Having told them this wonderful news, the king asked him three times—"Are you sure?" he said—"yes, I am sure." And said furthermore that if it is a lie, then they may kill him for telling a lie. Having confirmed it, the whole of them with their king from whose head the smoke was rushing out followed them to the place to witness this ground whether it is true. But as I had removed this head together with all the gifts and went away immediately he left there for the town, so when the whole of them followed him to the place, they did not see where the "ground has head and eyes" as he told them. But as he had been promised that they may kill him for telling a lie, so the king ordered the ghosts to kill him, because they did not see any sign of what he told them. This is how I took all my gifts back from him.

Of course, I did not return to the 18th town again, but started from there to find the way to my home town as usual, because that place was too far from the 18th town.

Television-handed Ghostess

When it was about 2 o'clock p.m. I saw a ghostess who was crying bitterly and coming to me direct in a hut where I laid down enjoying myself. When she entered I noticed that she held a short mat which was woven with dried weeds. She was not more than three feet high. Immediately she entered she went direct to the fire, she spread the mat closely to the fire and then sat down on it without saluting or talking to me. So at this stage I noticed carefully that she was almost covered with sores, even there was no single hair on her head, except sores with uncountable maggots which were dashing here and there on her body. Both her arms were not more than one and an half foot, it had uncountable short fingers. She was crying bitterly and repeatedly as if somebody was stabbing her with knives. Of course, I did not talk to her, but I was looking at her with much astonishment until I saw the water of her eyes that it was near to quench the fire, then I got up with anger and told her to walk out of my hut, because if the water quenches the fire I should not be able to get another again, as there were not matches in the Bush of Ghosts. But instead of walking out as I said she started to cry louder than ever. When I could not bear her cry I asked her—"by the way what are you crying for?" She replied

161

—"I am crying because of you." Then I asked again—
"because of me?" She said—"yes" and I said—"What
for?" Then she started to relate her story thus—

"I was born over two hundred years ago with sores on
my head and all over my body. Since the day that I was
born I have no other work more than to find out the
doctor who could heal it for me and several of them
had tried all their best but failed. Instead of healing
or curing it would be spreading wider and then giving
me more pains. I have been to many sorcerers to know
whether the sore would be healed, but every one of them
was telling me that there is an earthly person who had
been lost in this Bush of Ghosts, so that if I can be
wandering about I might see you one day, and the
sorcerers said that if you will be licking the sore every
day with your tongue for ten years it would be healed.
So that I am very lucky and very glad that I meet you
here today and I shall also be exceedingly glad if you will
be licking the sore with your tongue every day until the
ten years that it will be healed as the sorcerers had told
me. And I am also crying bitterly in respect of you because I believe that no doubt you have been struggling
for many years in this Bush of Ghosts for the right way to
your home town, but you are seeing the way every day
and you do not know it, because every earthly person gets
eyes but cannot see. Even it is on the right way to your
home town that you found this hut and sleep or sit in it
every day and night. Although I believe that you will
not refuse to lick the sore until it is healed."

Having related her story and said that if I am licking
the sore it would be healed as the sorcerers said, so I

replied—"I want you to go back to your sorcerers and tell them I refuse to lick the sore." After I told her like this she said again—"It is not a matter of going back to the sorcerers, but if you can do it look at my palm or hand." But when she told me to look at her palm and opened it nearly to touch my face, it was exactly as a television, I saw my town, mother, brother and all my playmates, then she was asking me frequently —"do you agree to be licking the sore with your tongue, tell me, now, yes or no?"

Hard to say "No" and
Hard to say "Yes"

Because when I thought over how the sore was dirty and smelling badly, especially those maggots which were dashing here and there all over the sore, so it was hard for me to say "yes". But as I was seeing my town with all my people, it was also hard for me to say "No". But as I was hearing on this television when my mother was discussing about me with one of her friends with a sorrowful voice at that time that—"She was told by a fortune teller that I am still alive in a bush." So as I was enjoying these discussions the television-handed ghostess took away the hand from my face and I saw nothing again except the hand.

After that she asked again whether I would do her request, of course, I was unable to answer at that moment, but only thinking about my people whom I saw on the television and also thinking how to reach the town as quickly as possible. But as it was just a dream for me, I told her again to let me look at them once more before I would answer her request. Immediately she showed it to me my people appeared again at the same time and as I was looking at them and also hearing what they were talking about me which I ought to answer if I was with

164

them, luckily, a woman brought her baby who had a sore on its foot to my mother at that time to tell her the kind of leaf which could heal the sore. But as my mother knows many kinds of leaves which can heal any sore, so she told this woman to follow her. Having reached a small bush which is near the town, then she cut many leaves on a kind of plant and gave them to this woman, after that she told her that she must warm the leaves in hot water before using it for the sore. But as I was looking at them on the television I knew the kind of leaf and also heard the direction how to use it. After a while this "Television-handed ghostess" took her hand away from my face and I saw nothing again. Then she asked again whether I would do her request, so I said—"Yes, but not with my tongue would I heal the sore." After I said "yes" I got out of the hut and I went round near the hut. God is so good, this kind of leaf or plant were full up there. Then I cut some and came back to the hut, after that I was using it for the sore according to the direction that my mother told the woman who brought her baby to her. It was so I was using these leaves for the sore every day and to my surprise, this sore had been healed within a week. But when this "Television-handed ghostess" saw that she had no more sores again she was exceedingly glad.

Having eaten and drunk to my satisfaction I told her to tell me the right way to my home town as she had promised me before I healed her sore. She agreed, but warned me seriously that I must not attempt to enter into the Bush of Ghosts forever, because 90% of ghosts hate any of the earthly persons to enter this bush, as I myself am aware of it since I have been struggling to find the right way back to my town, but none of the merciless ghosts would show me the way. After the above warning she said further—"Do not tell anybody that I am the 'Television-handed ghostess' who shows you the right way whenever you reach your town." Then she opened her palm as usual, she told me to look at it, but to my surprise, I simply found myself under the fruit tree which is near my home town (the Future-Sign). It was under this fruit tree my brother left me on the road when he was running away from the enemies' guns which were driving me farther and farther until I entered into the Bush of Ghosts, and it was the fruit of this tree I ate first immediately I entered the Bush of Ghosts. This is how I got out of the Bush of Ghosts, which I entered when I was seven years old.

The Future-Sign Tree

As I simply found myself under this fruit tree I stopped there for more than half an hour, because everything had been changed as before I left them. Of course, I believed that the fruit tree is near my town, otherwise I should not know at all that I am near my town. But as I stood under this fruit tree, thinking with doubtful mind that— "This fruit tree is marked as a 'Future-Sign' before I entered the bush" there I saw that two strong men held both my arms at my back unexpectedly and without hesitation they tied me with rope, then one of them put me on his head and both kept going inside the bush at the same time. They were slave-traders because the slave trade was then still existing.

After some days they reached their town which is foreign to mine. So having taken me to their town I was again sold to a man who took me to his town. But as there was no other transport to carry loads more than by head as now-a-days, so I was carrying heavy loads which three men could not carry at a time to long distances which I would travel for ten days with many other slaves. But as my body was full of sores, so it was debarring my boss getting loads from those who were giving him the job. For this reason he started to wash the sore of my body with a sponge and sand perhaps it would be healed and also flogging me severely if I cry or shake while he was washing the sore. Having done this every day for one month and when it was not healed, then he sold me again to another man who took me to the slave market, because I was not useful for any purpose in respect of the sore. Having reached the market he chained me to a tree together with the other slaves that we met there, all of us were in a straight line. But within four hours all the rest slaves had been sold and nobody buys me because of the sores. When he waited with me till about two o'clock and when he believed that no one could buy me that market day, then he was loosing the chain from me, and when he was about to return to his town a rich man came to the market, he looked round but saw no more slaves except me, because he kept late, then he came to my boss. He priced me very poor and my boss agreed, he told him to pay any amount that he likes to buy me, but when he stood before me and looked at me for many hours he said—"I cannot buy sores for my town." Then he went back to his town. But as nobody buys me and I remained unsold, so my boss was flogging me repeatedly along the way back to his town.

When he was taking me to this market for several market days without seeing anybody to buy me, then he said—"If I take you to the market once more and if nobody buys you on that market day as well so if I am returning from the market to the town I will kill you on the way and throw away your body into the bush, because you are entirely useless for any purpose, even I have told several of my friends to take you free of charge but none of them accepts the offer, because I can no longer remain with you and your sore which is smelling badly to everybody, even the smell is also disturbing my friends and all my customers to come to my house again before I bought you." But when the following market day was reached, the day he would kill me if there is nobody to buy me, luckily, this rich man came late to the market on that day as well, then he came to me because all the rest slaves had been sold, except me. When he came he asked from my boss how much he would sell me, but my boss told him to pay any amount that he likes. After he heard so, he stood looking at me for about an hour, then he looked round the market, but saw no more slaves, except me, then he said—"I will buy you, because I ought to sacrifice to my god with a slave for some months to come, so that I may kill you for the god." Having said so, he paid three shillings and sixpence to my boss and he received it from him with many thanks and also thanked God greatly that I leave him.

This is a great pity that I was lost in the Bush of Ghosts for twenty-four years with punishments and when I came out of it I am caught and sold again as a slave, and now a rich man buys me and he is going to kill me for his god. This is what I said before I was following him and his follower who followed him to the market was pushing me along the road to the town. Not knowing that this rich man is my brother who left me on the road and ran away before I entered the Bush of Ghosts. Having reached the town which is my town, they put me among his slaves in the yard, but the sore of my body still remained with me. So I was living and working with the rest slaves, but as this slave yard was far from his house he was only coming there occasionally to inspect us. But as he hated me more than the rest slaves because of the sore, so he would tell some of the rest slaves to flog me in his presence for many hours as I was not useful and also at that time it was their rule that every useless slave should be severely beaten every day, because every slave buyer recognised slaves as non-living creatures. Of course, I believed that I am in my town and my mother with my brother or my family are there also, but I did not know them again and they did not know me as well.

But in those days a slave is too common to approach his master or any of his master's family to talk or to discuss anything with him or her, so that I had no right to describe myself to my master who is my brother, that I am a native of that town and again it was hard to describe myself to the rest slaves because they were foreigners, I did not understand their language. But one day, when my mind was at rest my brother who is our master came to inspect us in the yard, as he was talking to us I listened to his voice well, and it was the same as before we left each other, again I looked at his forehead carefully which had a small scar before I left him and this scar was there as well, so through these two signs I believed that he is my brother, but still I was unable to talk to him at all, otherwise he would order the rest slaves to kill me on the same spot without hesitation.

One day, when I thought over that I am in my home town, but I could not see my family even I am a slave too in my town, so after a while I remembered the song which my brother and I were singing when we were eating the two slices of cooked yam which our mother left for us before she went to the market on the very day that we left each other, then I was singing this song and mentioning his name in this song several times. But as his name was mentioned, so whenever his wives were hearing the name they would be flogging me, and I did not understand what they were flogging me for. And as I was singing this sorrowful song every day, so one day, they reported me to him that—"Your slave who has sores on the body is mentioning your name whenever he is singing a kind of sorrowful song, hence all the slaves are strictly banned to mention their master's name." Having heard so he told them to go and bring me before him.

When I reached there and stood before him all my body was shaking and my voice was also trembling, because if a slave is selected from many slaves like this no doubt he is going to be killed for a god. Then he told me to repeat the song that I am singing in the yard so that he may hear it. His aim was to kill me on the same spot if I mention his name. But I started to sing this song and before I reached the part that his name should be mentioned he had remembered how we left ourselves on the road under the fruit tree. So at the same moment he shouted with gladness and jumped towards me. After that he told all his wives that I am his brother who had been lost twenty-four years ago. Then the second thing he did he told his orderlies to wash me, after that he brought many costly clothes for me as a king, but the sore of my body still remained there. After this his wives gave me food with drinks, then he sent for our mother and all his friends as well.

Gladness becomes Weeping

After a few minutes our mother came, but she did not know me again and I myself did not her as well, and it was this day I believed that "feeling" sometimes proves the same blood if they have left each other for long time that they are the same family, because my brother did not show me to our mother when she came, because he was waiting for his friends to come before he would tell her. So as she sat down behind me she was feeling perhaps I am her son. After a while my brother's friends came, they sat in the form of a circle and I was in the centre. Then my brother told the whole of us to kneel down to pray. After the prayer he told our mother that I am her son who had been lost since I was seven years old. But when our mother with my brother's wives with his friends heard so, all shouted with gladness and held me, but when they looked at my body and saw the sore they burst into a cry which lasted for about an hour before it stopped. And it was this day I believed that if "gladness is too much it sometimes becomes weeping". Having stopped crying our mother started to treat the sore and within a week willy-nilly it has been healed.

After the second day that my brother and mother knew me and I myself knew both of them as well, then he told me how he was captured. Our mother also told me how she was captured when coming home to rescue us immediately she heard from the market that war broke into the town. She said that she was captured and taken to a town of which she did not understand their language until she left there when resold to a lame woman. She said that the work that she was doing for the lame woman was only to be carrying her wherever she was going to, but she spent only four years with her before she sold her again on the way carrying her to somewhere, because she was feeling hunger and had no money to buy the food. So the lame woman gave mother to the food-seller and took food instead of paying her money. After she was exchanged to this food-seller, the food-seller was not feeding mother at all, so if she worked for her from early in the morning till eight o'clock in the night, then she would start to work from that night till dawn for her living, so by that she had no time at all to rest or sleep both day and night and she was doing so every day for years until she had a chance to escape at night, and again she was captured on the way by another man who was the most famous slave-buyer in his town. All his slaves were performing the same kind of work which only men could be performing, but however she was working as hard as a slave man. When her master noticed how she was working as a man, then he set her free after the 8th year that he captured her.

But when she came back to the town she met none of us in the town and was in a sorrowful life until my brother came after he spent many years in various towns. When he came both of us were expecting you every day to come home but it is in vain and they did not know

173

that it was in the Bush of Ghosts you were. Our mother told me as above. But one day when I remembered our dead cousin who I met in the 10th town of ghosts I told them about him that he had resettled down in a town in the Bush of Ghosts. I told them that I was educated from him because he had established schools and churches there. Of course when they heard so they were very surprised. They asked me whether I feared him as he had died in our town here in my presence before I left the town, so I replied that if anybody enters into the Bush of Ghosts he or her would not fear for anything within a week he or she had entered into it, because he or she will see "Fear" personally who bought the "Palm-Wine Drinker's" "fear" before he entered inside the "White-tree" to the "Faithful-mother". I told them further that it is in the Bush of Ghosts the "fears", "sorrows", "difficulties" all kinds of the "punishments" etc. start and there they end.

After that I hinted to them about the "SECRET-SOCIETY OF GHOSTS" which is celebrated once in every century. I told them that as it is near to be celebrated I like to be present there so that I may bring some of its news to them and other people. But when both of them heard so again from me, they said that I will not go to the Bush of Ghosts again in their presence. Of course they said this of their own accord, because I dreamed a dream that I am present when this "Secret Society of Ghosts" is performing and I believe so, because my dream always comes to the truth in future, however it may be. So you will hear about this news in due course.

"This is what hatred did."